Jean J. Jusserand

The Romance of a King's Life

Jean J. Jusserand

The Romance of a King's Life

ISBN/EAN: 9783337019969

Printed in Europe, USA, Canada, Australia, Japan

Cover: Foto ©Andreas Hilbeck / pixelio.de

More available books at **www.hansebooks.com**

The Romance

of

A King's Life

BY

J. J. JUSSERAND

TRANSLATED FROM THE FRENCH BY M. R.

REVISED AND ENLARGED BY THE AUTHOR

ILLUSTRATED

LONDON

T. FISHER UNWIN

1896

Alas for the woful thing
That a poet true and a friend of man
In desperate days of bale and ban
Should needs be born a king.

ROSSETTI.

TABLE OF CONTENTS.

7

LIST OF ILLUSTRATIONS.

———◦◦◦———

I.

GOING northwards, the landscape changes, meadows disappear, trees become scarcer, the sun grows dimmer. England leaves the impression of a huge park with rich verdure; Scotland the impression of a boundless moor covered as far as eye can see with heather. Beeches and larches thinly scattered on the edge of the streams project their irregular outlines against the dark background of the mountains. In those still solitudes, the clouds alone pursue their silent march across the sky; the wind sunders them, rolls them into flakes; they lower, halt on the hill-side, and seem to catch in the thorns; then free themselves, float lightly off, and are lost in the moving mass.

No sound, save the sound of waters; the brooks fall in cascades or quiver along the slopes; no song but the cawing of crows, gathered in

great bands, unscared by the passing of the
traveller ; they look without stirring, and the
most they do is to cease their chatter ; they are
at home and on their own ground, the passer-by
is the intruder. Winter soon comes with its
long nights ; a few hours after noon the shadows
lengthen, colder grows the air, darkness enshrouds
the moor, the pathway, the larches, and hardly
allows the traveller to see the light of the distant
hovel, marked out for the night's rest.

Dwellings are few and poor, built of irregular
stones without any mortar coating, and roofed in
with heather. Heather is the great friend ; without it human life would cease on the hills of
Scotland ; it gives the clear flame that warms the
hearth and lights the house, it forms the roof of
the abode, it affords material for the family couch
and the guest's bed ; its pink blossoms wrap the
landscape in beauty. Four walls of stone, and
a roof peaked on account of the snow, such is the
habitation ; oatmeal cakes, fish dried under the
chimney-board, such is the food ; the skin of a
long-haired calf spread on the clay floor, such is
comfort.

ˑ In these bare regions, beyond the lochs now
united by the Caledonian Canal, a land which
used to be known only by hearsay in Europe,
lived once what chroniclers called the " Wild

Scottis," or *catervani*, as they termed them
in their barbarous Latin. The race was a
proud and hardy one, delighting in dangers; the
men were soldiers, fishers, seamen; a deep feeling
of wondrous strength filled their breasts, the love
of their tribe; other sentiments had less hold
on them; the chief of the clan was to them the
incarnation of religion, country, and family, and
the chief acknowledged no master but God. No
law existed for those chiefs save that they made;
the royal laws were in their eyes foreign ones;
and it had ever been so. The Romans, masters
of the world, had given up trying to subdue the
people of Scotland, and in order not to draw back
themselves, had built in the north of England
the two famous walls going from one sea to the
other.

Through all the Middle Ages, the Scotch
remain the same. "They had as lief die," writes
of them Bartholomew the Englishman, "as be
in slavery, and say it is shameful to die in one's
bed. . . . Not often do they eat before the going
down of the sun. . . . And are an extremely
handsome people both in body and visage, but
wear a garb that does not make them look well."
Those who dwell near the border have left off
this garb; but "the wild Scots who live in the
woods take pride in keeping to their ancient

customs, in dress, in speech, and in their manner of life. . . . The Scots do not love peace." [1]

Thus, of all the hard trades plied in the rude Scotland of yore, the hardest was kingscraft. On the frontier, a truceless war ; the Roman walls have crumbled, and armies battle on their ruins ; within the frontier, the continual revolts, and the fratricidal strife of the *catervani* ; one single ally, distant France.

Over this land and this people reigned, in 1402, Robert III. Stuart. A strange doom rested on his race. The genius of the family, angel and demon by turns, appeared on birthdays to lay within the cradle crowns of gold, of flowers, or of laurel ; and the infant grew up brave and fair, a peerless poet, a lover of art, a sturdy soldier, to perish by the dagger, to mount the steps of the scaffold, or to die forgotten in the dismal palace of St. Germain in France.

The ramily had early a foreboding of its fate, and strove to appease the oracle. Robert III. in reality bore the name of John ; but it was an ill-omened one for a king, as had been seen with John of France, John of England, John of Bohemia, and John of Scotland. When the hour came for him to reign, he took the name of Robert ; but who can out-wit Fate ? All called

[1] See Appendix I.

him Robert, but Fate knew him as John of
Scotland, second of the name ; strange misfor-
tunes awaited him, a yet stranger fate awaited
his son.

II.

JAMES, son of Robert, was, in 1402, sole heir
to the old king. His life's tragedy had begun
early; he was only a boy when his elder brother
David, Duke of Rothesay, suffered imprisonment
at the hands of his uncle Robert Stuart, Duke of
Albany, who, it was rumoured, allowed the young
prince to die of hunger. James was sent, for his
early education, to Bishop Wardlaw, in the learned
and godly town of St. Andrews, and he lived for
a while in the episcopal castle, now a shapeless
ruin on a rocky headland, by the sea shore. The
child was in safety; but the king, always in fear
concerning the fate of the Stuarts, provoked
Destiny anew while trying to baffle her decrees.
He bethought himself of a better place to keep
the boy than St. Andrews, distant France;
there James would be secure from danger, would
study letters, and become an accomplished
knight.

16

BISHOPS' CASTLE, ST. ANDREWS.

The royal child put out to sea in the spring of 1405 ; it was a long journey. Froissart has told us how tedious time appeared on the ships of that period : the passengers used to play dice and make bets ; by way of diverting his companions a knight offered to climb in full armour to the top of the mast, his foot slipped, he fell into the sea, and he sank like a stone as may well be believed, which was a great pity. An unforeseen event shortened James's crossing ; as his vessel was passing off Flamborough Head, English sailors, warned it is thought by the traitor Albany, attacked the ship and carried away the passengers prisoners. The boarding took place on Palm Sunday, April 12, 1405 :

> This ilke schip sone takyn wes
> Ewyn upon the Palm sonday
> Before Pasch that fallis ay.

So says the contemporary chronicler, Andrew of Wyntoun. It was a time of peace ;[1] but was there ever real peace with Scotland? Henry IV. reigned at Westminster Palace ; a self-willed and unscrupulous prince, he deemed that what was good to take was good to keep ; he had applied this maxim to the kingdom of England, and

[1] Appendix II.

acting upon it had deposed, imprisoned, and put
to death his predecessor and cousin, Richard II.
He therefore did not hesitate to send James to
the Tower, and was so little troubled in his
conscience that the only remark the event
elicited from him was : " If the Scotch had
been good people they would have sent me this
young man to teach, for I too know French very
well." [1]   A captivity of eighteen years began
for the heir of the Stuarts.

> Stone walls do not a prison make,
> Nor iron bars a cage ;

the mind of the child fast growing to man-
hood was never captive. Behind the thick walls
of the Tower, built in former times by the
Conqueror, he studied ; guards watched over
him, but his spirit was afar, and journeyed in
the realms of poetry. Thus he visited in his
imaginary travels, heavy books on his knee, by
the light of his casement, the famous fields where
the deeds of the Romans were performed ; he
went to the plain of Troy, and beheld what
was then to be seen there, knights in armour
slaying each other for the love of Helens in

---

[1] " Certe si grati fuerint Scoti, hunc misissent mihi juvenem
instituendum, nam et idioma Franciæ ego novi." Walsingham,
" Historia Anglicana," Rolls, ii. p. 273.

cornets. The noble senator Boethius taught
him resignation; Guillaume de Lorris took his
hand and led him to the Garden of the Rose;
illustrious Chaucer beckoned him to join, on the
Canterbury road, the noisy troop of his pilgrims;
sober Gower, announcing beforehand a sermon of
several hours, begged him to be seated, and to
the sound of his wise words the child, with his
head thrown back on the window-sill, quietly
slept.

Thus passed the years, and the main change
they brought was a change of prison; after
the Tower the keep of Nottingham, another
Norman citadel; then Evesham, then the Tower
again at the accession of Henry V., Windsor
Castle, the Tower once more, Kenilworth,
Pontefract, and other fortresses.

From time to time came tidings from abroad,
mostly evil ones; fate continued adverse to the
prisoner. Then dark hours began for him;
" Bel Accueil " smiled in vain; the mirth of
the Canterbury pilgrims was no longer catching;
the Trojan war lost its fascination; the boy
dreamed of other wars.

Fortune did not tire of befriending the English;
they now had a whole " treasury " of prisoners
representing every hostile nation. There were,
besides James of Scotland, Gruffyd, son of the

famous Welsh rebel Owen Glendower, as the
English called him, unable to pronounce his real
name of Glyndyfrdwy; Murdoch Stuart, Earl of
Fife, another Scot, son of Albany, and who had
preceded James at the Tower, having been made
prisoner at Homildon Hill; and finally, the
princely poet, Charles of Orléans, who came in
1415 to tell the other captives of the disaster at
Agincourt. Fortune continued to be opposed to
France and her ally; the epos of the " Bonne
Lorraine " had not yet begun.

Sadder than all others were the tidings from
Scotland. On hearing of his son's misfortune,
the old king had been seized with so deep a grief
that he declined from day to day. He refused at
last all food, and died on Palm Sunday, 1406, the
anniversary of his sorrow.[1] He had requested to
have graven on his tomb : " Here lies the worst

> [1] A thousand and four hundyr yere
>   To tha the sext all reknyt clere,
>   Sanct Ambrose fest in till Aprile
>   The ferd day fallis, bot in that quhile
>   That fest fell on Palm Sunday,
>   The quhilke before Pasch fallis ay,
>   Robert the Thrid, oure Lord the King,
>   Maid at Dundownald his endyng.

Andrew of Wyntoun, " Orygynale Cronykil," ed. Laing, vol. iii.
p. 98. As Andrew states it, the feast of St. Ambrose and Palm
Sunday happened on the same day, April 4, in the year 1406.

of kings and the unhappiest of men." [1] Fate had never forgotten that Robert III. was in truth John of Scotland. At the king's death, the traitor Albany had become regent. He despatched occasional embassies to England for the deliverance of his nephew ; the envoys always failed in their mission, and were no less favourably looked upon by their master. He also sent missions for the liberation of his son Murdoch, but these met with better success ; Murdoch returned to his own land, leaving James a prisoner, a fact kept in mind by the youthful prince, in whom began to stir the vengeful spirit of the Stuarts.

[1] " . . . Ut scribatis pro meo epitaphio : Hic jacet pessimus rex et miserrimus hominum in universo regno." Bower, in his continuation of Fordun's " Scotichronicon," 1759, vol. ii. p. 441.

III.

POETS have celebrated in their epic tales, illuminators have painted in their gold-adorned miniatures, the prisoner of war, confined in a dungeon on the banks of the Thames or the Rhône, in the Tower of London or at Beaucaire, or in the land of poetry and dreams. The captive leans sadly out of the narrow window of his cell ; he sees the silent river flow ; he hears the clash of lances and of armour ; military bands are starting on an expedition ; then, again, it is spring time and dawn ; flowers bathed in dew turn towards the rising sun ; birds carol in the groves at the foot of the tower ; and here comes through the wet grass, blithe as the birds, fresh as the flowers, or pensive sometimes and full of thoughts, the maiden seen in dreams, the giver of joy or sorrow. Beholding his vision realised, the prisoner doubts whether he be awake or asleep. The maiden treads the paths, stoops to pluck the flowers, sits in the shade of the trees while the sun mounts ; in her turn she dreams.

She is called Nicolette in the tale of Aucassin, Emily in Chaucer's "Knight's Tale," she was called Jane Beaufort in the romance of real life lived by James of Scotland.

Jane belonged, as did the prisoner, to a race of tragic destinies, the Somersets, a branch of the royal family of Lancaster, the chief scions of which were, for over a hundred years, slain in war or beheaded for high treason. Jane's brother fell on the field of St. Albans, two of her nephews perished on the scaffold, the third was killed at Tewkesbury; one of her grand-nephews won the battle of Bosworth and became King Henry VII.

She appeared one day under the walls of James's prison, young and fair as a heroine of romance, with an air both gentle and resolute. The prince saw her from his window, coming as the maidens in miniatures to gather flowers in the dew, at the foot of the gloomy walls. Never had James seen anything so charming save in imagination, while turning the pages of his favourite Chaucer. Youth stood before him, Beauty, and all the wondrous beings with which the authors of that time liked to people their palaces of love. James became enamoured, made his passion known, had the joy of seeing it shared; he sang it.

IV.

LIKE most of the Stuarts, the captive king was a poet. He was also a musician, an artist, an excellent horseman and tennis-player; he was skilful in all things. After he knew Jane Beaufort, love gilded the bars of his prison, and life changed its aspect; the world for him was an immense parterre where Jane gathered flowers, the rest was non-existent; the abstractions of the Garden of the Rose took shape in his eyes, his soul was no longer lonely, he conversed with Bel Accueil, he defended himself against Male-Bouche, he took counsel of Venus and of Minerva; the fancies of rhymers were no longer fancies to him, books of love no longer poetic pastimes; the rose of love was no longer an allegory; his rose was a living rose, with bright eyes, scarlet lips, and a heart that beat; she had a name and a rank in the world; James loved Jane Beaufort.

He sang Jane Beaufort. He sang her according to the fashion of the day, in musical and delightful verses, verses full of birds and flowers, where we seem continually to hear the flutter of wings, where the branches rustle softly in the morning breeze, where spring-tide sets the seal of youth on brow and heart. Jane is represented in the " Kingis Quair " [1] like a figure in a manuscript, slight, tall, graceful ; and—love works these marvels—after four hundred years she has not been frozen by death ; her hands retain their warmth.

But how differently were told, in a style peculiar to the period, joys and sorrows like unto ours !

> Heigh in the hevynnis figure circulere
> The rody sterres twynklyng as the fyre ;
> And, in Aquary, Cynthia the clere
> Rynsid hir tressis like gold in wyre . . .

in other words it was night. Instead of sleeping the poet-king mused ; he recalled his woes, he thought of his country, and of that persistent enmity of Fate which, after so many years, continued to keep him away from his own hearth. He opened a book, the book opened by all

[1] " The Kingis Quair," ed. by W. W. Skeat, Scottish Text Society, 1883–4.

the wretched of former days, and which, in that
time when sudden reverses overtook even the
strongest, had been translated into all the lan-
guages of Europe, the *Consolation* of Boethius,

> that noble senatoure
> Off Rome, quhilom that was the warldis floure.

James was still reading when he heard in the
air outside the sound of the matin bell :

> Bot now, how trowe ye ? suich a fantasye
> Fell me to mynd, that ay me thoght the bell
> Said to me, " Tell on, man, quhat the befell."

How disobey a bell ?   He therefore seated himself at the table where he had already wasted
much "ink and paper, spent to lyte effect,"
took a pen, made a cross on the first page, and
thus began. . . .

He begins by addressing the Muses, an elegant fashion which was not then as antiquated
as it has become since ; he invokes Clio and
Polymnia like Chaucer, and adds "Thesiphone,"
whom he takes for a muse, being less versed in
mythology than Chaucer.   He is going to relate
all that happened to him,

> to write my turment and my joye.

Firstly about his childhood ; his departure from
Scotland,

With mony " fare wele " and " Sanct Johne to borowe,"

wishes of loving friends, not granted by Fortune;
then comes the episode of his capture at sea, and
the description of his years of exile, the weary
days, the wearier nights.

One morning, early risen as was his wont out
of love for the sweet hours of dawn, he leaned
at his window; it was one of his amusements.
He enjoyed watching from there :

> To se the warld and folk that went forby ;
> As for the tyme, though I of mirthis fude
> Myght have no more, to luke it did me gude.

He looked out on a garden, quite green and full
of flowers; the nightingale sang, and the words
of her song seemed to be :

> Worschippë, ye that loveris bene, this may,
>   For of your blisse the kalendis are begonne,
> And sing with us : Away, winter, away !
>   Cum, Somer, cum, the suete sesoun and sonne !

And as the youthful king cast down his eyes,
what should he see, save what he took for a
living flower,

> The fairest or the freschest yongë floure
> That ever I sawe, me-thoght, before that houre.

The blood rushed to his heart, and he suddenly

drew back from the window, as if he had seen
something he should not, and at once bent his
head again towards the garden :

> sudaynly my hert became hir thrall
> For ever, of free wyll ; for of menace
> There was no takyn in hir suetë face.

Thus James loved Jane at first sight and for
ever, as Theagenes had loved Chariclea, and as
Des Grieux will love Manon. "Je m'avançai
vers la maîtresse de mon cœur," Des Grieux
says when he has just caught a first glimpse of
Manon. The Greek heroes in the same way
had looked on each other's faces, and read in
each other's eyes so deep a love that they could
not believe it born on the spot, and wondered
where they had met before. " A ! suete," cries
James,

> ar ye a warldily creature,
> Or hevinly thing in likenesse of nature ?
> Or ar ye god Cupidis owin princesse,
>   And cummyn are to louse me out of band ?
> Or ar ye verray Nature the goddesse
>   That have depaynted with your hevinly hand
>   This gardyn full of flouris as they stand ?
> Quhat sall I think, allace ! quhat reverence
> Sall I minister to your excellence ?

He does not weary of gazing and worshipping ;
he admires her hair, her attire, her hands, her face

fair "eneuch to mak a world to dote"; enough to "ramener l'univers à l'idolâtrie," as Des Grieux will say in nearly the same words three hundred years later, so greatly does love resemble love.

James cannot take his eyes off her; he prays, he beseeches, he sings; he watches the slightest motions of the maiden, her gait, the folds of her gown; he is silent, then talks anew and his words are like caresses; we know that he will find out the way to touch her and win his suit:

> Yif ye a goddesse be, and that ye like
> To do me payne, I may it noght astert.

He envies the little dog whose bell tinkles along the path, in front of her. She departs, and it seems to him that the flowers close, and the day declines. Never had the prison walls seemed so oppressive; he remains near the window whence he can see out; he kneels on the stone, he stares into vacant space,

> Till Phebus endit had his bemes bryght
> And bad go farewele every lefe and floure.

Night has come, and yet he still remains there; he dozes on the window-ledge.

Half sleeping, half waking, he has a dream. No work of imagination or of sentiment would

then have been complete without a dream.   He
fancies himself in the palace of the goddess
Venus, mistress of his destiny ; the palace is
filled with the lovers of old, rewarded by endless
joy for having suffered the pangs of love ; princes,
poets, " yong folkis ; "

> Here bene the princis, faucht the grete batailis
> In mynd (memory) of quhom ar maid the bukis newe ;

here .are those who were ashamed of being
in love, whose service to the goddess was
" cowardy " ; they are allowed within the palace,
because after all they were lovers, but

> For schame thaire hudis ovre thaire eyne thay hyng.

James holds love, as others have done since,
to be a religion and a virtue, its devotees merit
paradise—" que la terre leur soit légère ! "
    There the poet-king meets Fair-Calling and
all his friends of the Romaunt of the Rose ;
Cupid, " the blynd god,"

> And on his longë yalow lokkis schene
> A chaplet had he all of levis grene.

He carries his golden bow, and his harmful
arrows. Venus reclines on her couch, her head
is decked with flowers :

A FIFTEENTH CENTURY REPRESENTATION OF THE STAR GODDESS VENUS.

And on hir hede, of rede rosis full suete
A chapellet sche had, faire, fresch, and mete.

She wore a mantle—

A mantill caste over hir schuldris quhite,

a piece of apparel that Chaucer, less modest,
had neglected to place on them. Be merciful,
" Quene of Lufe! sterre of benevolence!" and
the king in tears tells his sorrow; he longs to
behold once more the maiden of the garden ; if
he does not see her again he will die. Listen,
" O bryght, blisfull goddesse,"

And with the stremes of your percyng lyght
    Convoy my hert, that is so wo-begone,
Ageyne unto that suete hevinly sight
    That I, within the wallis cald as stone,
    So suetly saw on morow walk and gone,
Law in the gardyn, ryght tofore myn eye :
Now, merci, Quene ! and do me noght to deye.

And the goddess takes pity on him. She knows
how to cure the wounds inflicted by her son :

He can the stroke, to me langis (belongs) the cure.

I shall heal thine if thou pledgest thy word to
love for ever, and to teach my law to men,

Quhen thou descendis doun to ground ageyne.

For men forego my empire and love no more;
this thought wounds my " wofull tender hert ";
I weep,

> And of my cristall teris that bene schede,
> The hony flouris growen up and sprede
> That preyen men [as] in thaire flouris wise,
> Be trewe of lufe, and worschip my servise.

A Venus in a "mantill" is not an ordinary
Venus; no wonder that this one, giving the
poet " Gude-Hope " for a guide, sends him to
Minerva, a precaution the Venus of Titian
might perhaps have omitted. The Goddess of
Wisdom shows herself most prudent; her advice
is drawn from the book of all wisdom; she
agrees on every point with King Solomon; too
honest to conceal it, she admits that she's merely
quoting passages from *Ecclesiastes*: the poet is
again visiting a goddess unknown to Olympus.
He promises, " be Him that starf (died) on rude,"
to love, to be ever true, and to do anything he
be ordered; but, "madame," allow me to see
her again,

> To sene the fresche beautee of hir face.

Well instructed in his duty the king leaves
Minerva, who pierces with a ray the immensity
of clouds, and forms a shining track by which

THE WHEEL OF FORTUNE, FIFTEENTH CENTURY.

he descends to earth. He finds himself on the
border of a stream,

Embroudin all with fresche flouris gay ;

whose waters ripple over golden pebbles ; in its
eddies swim fish with ruby scales. Following
the river he meets the Goddess Fortune, who,
seeing his "dedely couloure pale," has pity on
him, and just as she promises he shall know the
highest place in her terrible wheel, the prince
opens his eyes and finds himself still leaning on
his window ; below him the garden awakes,
above him the sun rises.

Is it a dream ? And if so, where does it
begin ? Can its most beautiful part, the appearance of Jane Beaufort, be only mist ? Mist,
like the palace of Venus ? mist, like Minerva
quoting Ecclesiastes, and like the river with
ruby fish ? The real and unreal mingle ; the
poet sees, or thinks he sees ; he is awake, and yet
the dream goes on ; through his casement, open
to the morning breeze, a snow-white dove has
just entered ; she drops before the lover a sprig
of red gillyflower ; is it another illusion ? or do
his eyes really perceive golden letters upon the
green stalk ? And these letters say :

Awak ! awake ! I bring, lufar (lover), I bring
The newis glad, that blisfull ben and sure

> Of thy confort ; now lauch, and play and syng,
> That art besid so glad an aventure,
> For in the hevyn decretit is the cure.

Is it not wonderful ? Less wonderful though than the sight of Jane Beaufort in the garden.

Blessed be, thinks the king, the starry goddesses that shine in the sky,

> So fair that glitteren in the firmament ;

blessed be the Goddess Fortune, notwithstanding her terrible slippery wheel ; blessed be the nightingale, whose love-song has delighted the heart of her I love ; blessed be the gillyflower above all other flowers ; blessed be all flowers because of the gillyflower ; blessed be the walls of the prison where I was visited by these heavenly visions. Some will perhaps say that it is making much ado for a vain trifling fancy ; but they are wrong. Think of a man who has crept from hell to heaven ; could he keep silent ? Every man has his mind full of " his own sweet or sore " :

> Bot for als moche as sum micht think or seyne
> Quhat nedis me, apoun so litill evyn,
> To writt all this ? I ansuere thus ageyne :
> Quho that from hell war croppin onys in hevin,
> Wald after o thank for joy mak sex or sevin ;
> And every wicht his awin suete or sore
> Has maist in mynde : I can say you no more.

Silence befits only those who are staggered by
the dangers on the road,

> And has no curage at the rose to pull.

Go little book, " nakit of eloquence,"

> Unto [the] impnis of my maisteris dere
>   Gowere and Chaucere, that on the steppis satt
> Of rethorike quhill thai were lyvand heie,
>   Superlative as poetis laureate
>   In moralitee and eloquence ornate,
> I recommend my buk in lynis sevin,
> And eke thair saulis unto the blisse of hevin.   Amen.[1]

[1] Appendix III.

V.

VENUS, Minerva, and the dove with the gillyflower had told the truth, better days were in store. Even in Scotland the future seemed less dark ; death had put an end to the regency of Albany ; Murdoch, his heir, could not long continue his father's policy and thwart the nation's desire to have back its king. In her turn England was under tutelage, and knew the evils of long minorities ; the hero of Agincourt slept now among his peers on the threshold of the Confessor's Chapel, his hauberk and helmet, worn in the French wars, lay, idle trophies, beneath an arch of Westminster, where they still remain. The hour draws near when the " King of Chinon " will be " Charles le Victorieux."

An embassy arrived from Scotland, this time with orders to succeed ; in the summer of 1423 the delegates of both countries came to an agreement. James was to pay a ransom of sixty thousand gold marks. The contract was signed on the 10th of September in the Chapter House at York. The King of Scotland was free.

Before returning to his country the king's dream was realised. One morning in the month of February, 1424, the Church of St. Mary Overy, on the other side of London Bridge, was decked as for a festival, the chimes sounded their merry peals; they did not say like the matin bell, "Tell thy woes," they rang out the joy of the poet-king. That day, in the church where one of his masters in poetry, Gower, a chaplet of roses on his brow, lay buried, James Stuart, henceforth James I. of Scotland, was wedded to Jane Beaufort.

They started at once for their dominions, and on the 21st of May were anointed at Scone, still held by the Scots a holy city, even now that the English had removed the famous Jacob's stone, another trophy kept at Westminster. The aged Bishop Wardlaw, who had not seen his pupil since the day, nineteen years ago, when so many "Fare wele" and "Sanct Johne to borowe" were exchanged, placed the crown on the king's head. Great was the enthusiasm throughout the land; the nobles vied with each other in offering themselves as hostages for the payment

of the ransom. James gave nine thousand
marks towards it. Precise minds will regret to
hear that having made this effort, the royal poet
did not go further, and never paid a single mark
of the remainder : so that long after his death
the poor hostages continued to do penance in
England, waiting for a ransom that never came.

Dire was the state of the kingdom : the weak
government of Robert III., the tyranny and
partiality of Albany, had stirred up the spirit of
rebellion ; lawlessness was at its height. The
chiefs of the clans governed their own men and
acknowledged no master ; each had few subjects,
but his rule was undisputed. The national
forces had no cohesion, there was no centralisation, no obedience to a supreme authority ; clans
waged war with one another regardless of the
fatherland's welfare, and no more importance was
attached to these wars than if they had been
private duels. What could be done in this rude
country by a dreamer scarce out of fairyland,
suddenly called upon to ply the hard trade of
kingscraft ?

Strange as it may appear, the poet of Fair-
Calling and of Good-Hope seemed trans-
formed from the moment he set foot on his
native soil. His affection for his beloved Jane
continues undiminished, but there is room for

an iron will besides; he meditates, matures plans, remembers what he has seen in other countries—in France, where Henry V. had taken him for a time; and in England, at Westminster and London. The stern chiefs of the "catervani" discovered in him a will more indomitable than their own; unfortunately his will would possess his whole mind so that he could see nothing either to the right or to the left but only his appointed goal, taking no difficulties or impossibilities into account—a common but fatal characteristic of the Stuart race. "I want," he had said in proud words, on the day he crossed the frontier, "the key to keep the castle and the bush to keep the cow." [1] All his life's energy was to be spent in the pursuit of that impossible aim.

Before all things the kingdom was to be regulated; external peace was indispensable. James maintained it throughout his whole reign; Jane helped him to keep it with England, even though the old alliance with France remained unbroken. He put an end to the ancient broils commercial jealousies had stirred up between the Flemings and the Scots. He reduced and settled the tribute his kingdom owed Norway

---

[1] Bower's continuation of Fordun's "Scotichronicon," Edinburgh, 1759, vol. ii. p. 511.

for the islands since the distant date of their conquest by the Scandinavian Vikings.[1]

During his stay among the English, James had been struck by the utility and effectiveness of that system then unique in the world—the Parliament sitting at Westminster. Every lever needs a fulcrum, and he felt that a parliament was the fulcrum best suited to a king. His decision once taken, he proceeded without delay to act upon it. He developed the representative institutions of the kingdom, and was careful to have his reforms ratified from year to year by his Parliament. Henceforth the laws imposed on the chiefs of clans would not be merely the laws of the king, but the laws of all the nation. By this means the prince was enabled to exact more, and he did not fail of doing so : all his laws have centralisation, organisation, and peaceful development for their object. All feuds are punished whether civil, religious, or military ; the unruliness of the " Wild Scottis " in particular is met by stern measures.

Parliaments succeed each other at Perth, Stirling, and Edinburgh : they decide, with the king's consent, that private wars shall be prohibited ; those who neglect to aid the sovereign in his expeditions against the rebels shall be held

[1] Appendix IV.

as rebels themselves ; the highland chieftains, instead of dwelling where they please, must restore and inhabit their dilapidated manors ; it will thus be possible to know where to find them, and they will be responsible for good order in their district. James sets the example by repairing the tower of Inverness and his other strongholds. He encourages artillery, which supplies the sovereign with a power not wielded by his subjects ; he has a cannon sent from Flanders, *the Lion*, "machinam bombardicam vocatam Lyoun," [1] the largest yet seen in Scotland. The king and Parliament forbid the chiefs to travel with those numerous retinues which resembled armies and allowed of skirmishes resembling battles. Laws shall be codified ; royal shall replace local justice. Heretics shall be carefully burned.

Salmon, a staple article of trade in Scotland, is protected by special laws ; smoked it was exported in barrels to England and the Continent ; merchants who brought foreign goods to Scotland were often paid partly in money and partly in salted salmon.[2] War shall be waged on those immense flocks of rooks who devour the young corn ; the heather must not be set on fire, as in

---

[1] "Liber Pluscardensis," 1877, vol. i. p. 376, year 1431.

[2] "Exchequer Rolls of Scotland," vol. iv. p. cxlv.

this way the crops may be destroyed. Small
landholders will be protected against the great.
All men will practise archery from twelve years
old and upwards. Football is not to be played
any more : this was coming very near un-
sufferable tyranny.[1]

James suspected as much, and, unable to rule
it, he dreaded the inherited spirit of the Stuarts.

Lat wisedome ay to thy will be iunyt,

had been the timely warning given him by the
Goddess Minerva. But James was not the
master of his own will. He did not see his goal
as it was, but he saw it surrounded with such
a halo that he became blind to all dangers. No
prince evinced more cruelty in his vengeance
than the poet of the gold-lettered gillyflowers ;
it seems as if the hatreds of Rimini or Ferrara
had been transplanted to northern climes.

The house of Albany has fomented strife : it
must be crushed. Its chiefs and their principal
adherents are arrested and delivered up to Parliament : for the example of respect to that body

---

[1] On these various laws see Appendix V. The statute on
football foresees the case in which the lord of the land (a most
probable case) would refuse to receive the fine to which tres-
passers would be sentenced.

must be set by the king himself. Parliament condemns them ; Murdoch, the former companion in years of exile, is beheaded ; his sons Walter and Alexander are also beheaded. Pity was felt for them "because they were such fine fellows and of such tall stature" ("homines giganteæ staturæ"). The aged Earl of Lennox, Murdoch's father-in-law, nearly eighty, is likewise executed ; five others are drawn, "equis tracti," and their quartered bodies nailed to the gibbets of the principal towns in Scotland. Death was held of such small account in those days that tortures or infamy were joined to it that it should not pass unnoticed.

The highland chieftains, disregarding the commands of king and Parliament, continued to fight together at will. Lost in their ravines, sheltered by their hills and bogs, hidden in their islands, they went on acknowledging no master but God. James mustered his forces, mounted his horse, met the "catervani" on the shore of one of their lochs, cut them in pieces, and drowned them in the loch ; but next year the scattered clans had resumed shape again, fierce and independent as before. The king had not secured his end ; he had to find other means, no matter which, as he *must* secure it. The royal poet therefore assembled at Inverness the

chieftains, "one by one with great wisdom," [1]
remarks the good monk Walter Bower, a contemporary chronicler, who knew James person-
ally many years ; and when they were all come
into his tower he singled out fifty of them,
beheaded a MacArthur, hanged a Campbell
and several others, and imprisoned the remainder
—all without a frown, and without in the least
troubling himself about a possible vengeance,
keeping his even temper so perfectly that he
improvised, by way of defiance, a Latin epigram
(with a false quantity) on this dismal deed :

> Ad turrim fortem ducamus caute cohortem ;
> Per Christi sortem, meruerunt hi quia mortem.

But the goal was not to be reached ; the
attempt of James was premature.   The first
thing Angus Murray did, on leaving prison, was
to send a challenge to Angus Macduff, chief of
the Mackays of Strathnavern.   They met, but
not singly, each chief had a following of twelve
hundred men strictly told ; and so fierce was the
struggle, the sense of honour so high, and flight
held for so shameful, that only nine survived.

[1] " Quorum unumquemque sagaciter et singillatim invitavit ad
turrim, et seorsum in arcta poni fecit custodia."   Year 1427 ;
Bower, in his continuation of Fordun's " Scotichronicon," 1759,
vol. ii. p. 489.

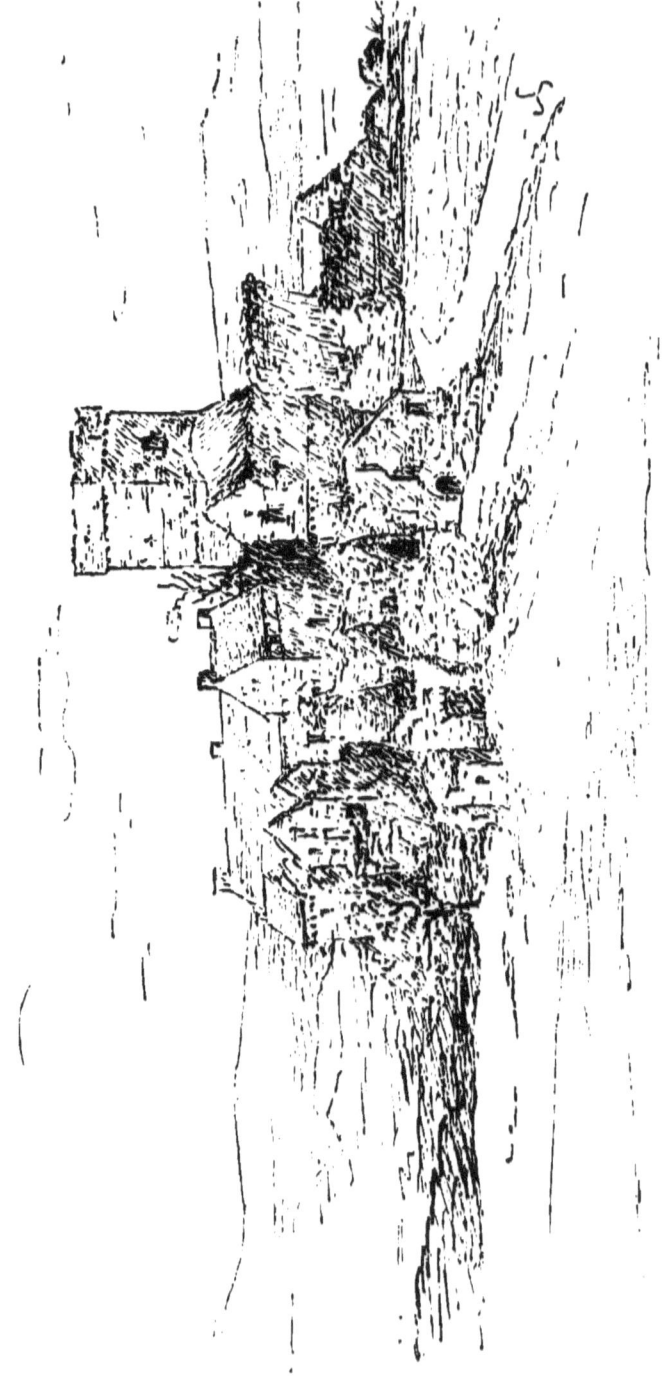

RUINS OF INCHCOLM.

This is attested again by Bower, who says that it is a wonderful fact, but yet a fact. " The Scottish highlanders," he remarks, by way of funeral oration for the slaughtered *catervani*, " living on the confines and marches of the world, are by nature more audacious than other nations." [1]

Alexander, Lord of the Isles, had also been imprisoned, then set at liberty, leaving his own mother as hostage ; she was confined in the abbey of Inchcolm under the guard of this same Bower, the chronicler. Once free, the Lord of the Isles gathers his clans, marches against the royal town of Inverness, takes and burns it. James is compelled to collect his troops and wage war in person against his subject. He pursues and overtakes him in the morasses of Lochaber, " in quodam marisco de Lochaber " (1429). The *catervani* are routed and scattered ; clan Chattan and clan Cameron join the royal banner ; the Lord of the Isles sues for peace, which is refused. The king triumphs.

On the eve of St. Augustine-the-Doctor was witnessed in the chapel of Holy Rood a moving sight. Wearing only a shirt, a halter round his neck, holding his sword by the point, a suppliant passed up the nave, and stopping

[1] Appendix VI.

before the king's throne proffered him his weapon.
It was Alexander, Lord of the Isles, the descen-
dant of the famous Somerlaed, the heir to the
Scandinavian kings, who was begging for mercy.
James had given few proofs of clemency, and the
fate of the rebel seemed certain ; the gibbets of
the four towns awaited his quartered body. But
Jane was present ; she besought the king to
pardon, and James granted the prayer he read in
the eyes of his love. The Lord of the Isles
received the boon of his life, and was imprisoned
in the castle of Tantallon.

That order might also reign in matters
spiritual, and to keep his subjects in the narrow
way that leads to heaven, James made severe war
on the Wyclifites, Hussites, and all other heretics.
Paul Crawar of Prague, " hæreticus obstinatus,"
come over to preach the doctrines of Hus, was
seized and burned with great solemnity by way
of warning, in the town of St. Andrews. He
persisted to the last in denying Purgatory and
the Resurrection of the Dead.

VI.

IN our days, a prince who should have the bloody limbs of his foes gibbeted on the public square, would be considered cruel; he would doubtless be so even in his own eyes, and his life would be disturbed by the thought of vengeance to be dreaded, or retaliation prepared. Small leisure would be left him for the delights of family life, or the enjoyment of art.

It was not so formerly : the fierce, warlike ruler of the Scots was still the poet of the "Kingis Quair"; he continued to write verses, and remained the impassioned lover of Jane Beaufort. Even in the laws of the kingdom traces of his fondness are to be seen : the Scots shall offer up prayers in their churches not only for the king, but for the queen likewise ; besides the oath of allegiance to the king, a personal

oath of allegiance shall be taken to the queen.[1]
Heaven had blessed the marriage, and many
children grew up around the royal couple :
Margaret, ·Isabel, James, afterwards king, Jane,
Eleanor, Mary, Anabella.   On his return home
after his raids, the prince became once more the
poet of the " Kingis Quair " ; he displayed the
amiability and liveliness of the Stuarts ; he
chatted late into the night, read romances,
played chess.   Seated by the queen under the tall
mantelpiece, piling logs on the fire, either in the
Perth monastery or in the castle of Linlithgow,
the favourite abode of Queen Jane (and the
future birthplace of Mary Queen of Scots), he
liked to tell tales of yore ; sometimes he recited
verses, or made music : he was wholly a Stuart.
But, differing in this from all other Stuarts, he
proved himself as true as tender ; almost alone
of his race, he never had a mistress ; he did not
follow the example of his ancestors, of Robert II.

---

[1] " Dominus rex noster, ex deliberatione et consensu tocius con-
silii statuit quod omnes et singuli successores prelatorum regni
quorumcumque necnon omnes et singuli heredes futuri comitum,
baronum omniumque liberetenencium domini Regis teneantur
facere consimile juramentum domine nostre Regine ; nec ullus
prelatus de cetero admittatur ad suam temporalitatem aut heres
cujusvis tenentis domini Regis ad suas tenandrias nisi prius prestet
regine illud juramentum." Perth Parliament of 1428. " Acts
of the Parliament of Scotland," vol. ii.

LINLITHGOW.

for example, who left eight bastards besides fourteen legitimate children.

His voice was fine, and he played, moreover,
on many instruments, such as the cittern, organ,
flute, and even the trumpet. He resembled
Orpheus, says Bower, who adds with more
truth : " he was a true Scot." [1] He also drew
fine miniatures, and doubtless depicted more than
once the romance lived by him in England, the
gloomy walls of the citadel, the prisoner at his
window, the maiden treading the garden paths
and picking flowers in the dew. Such a subject
was a favourite one with painters, and several
representations of it are still extant, but none by
the King of Scotland. One of them shows us a
fellow exile of his, like him, too, a poet, Charles
of Orléans, at the window of the Tower of
London, sadly watching the waters of the
Thames flowing towards the sea, towards liberty
and fair France.[2]

In the day time, when not engaged in war-
fare, James indulged his fondness for physical
sports. He was an excellent tennis player, and
on fine days endless matches took place between
him and his friends in the moat of the monastery

[1] Appendix VII.
[2] Reproduced as a frontispiece for my " Literary History of the
English People."

at Perth, where he liked to withdraw. He
threw the hammer better than any one, and
drew a straight and strong bow, rarely missing
his aim : " Optimus arcitenens et hastiludior
gnarus ; ultra communem usum hominum lapidis
jactor et mallei projector." Excelling in horsemanship, scarcely a noticeable accomplishment
in an age when horsemanship was a necessity, he
practised running and walking as distinct arts ;
he seemed to have " wings to his heels," and
prided himself on being one of the best pedes-
trians in the kingdom.

His religious zeal was not confined to burning
Paul Crawar ; he built chapels, and founded a
monastery in his favourite town of Perth. Great
surprise was expressed on learning what religious
order he intended to establish there : the con-
templative order of the Carthusians ; this choice
was much criticised. " I have been told," writes
Bower, " that many speak ill of this holy order
because they have never heard of miracles wrought
by Carthusians, whereas members of all other
holy orders perform them." But this is not at
all surprising : " The Carthusians, desirous of
pleasing God only, carefully conceal the miracles
wrought by them, and therefore to doubt the
sanctity and purity of the order is not only sacri-
legious but blasphemous as well." Who doubts

the holiness of John the Baptist ? " Know you,
that miracles are commonly wrought to prove
the holiness of he who performs them when
doubt is possible," and for this reason " John the
Baptist performed never a one, though no son
of woman was greater than he." James, in
accordance with these somewhat contradictory
reasons, founded his monastery at Perth, in the
Vale of Virtues, and it was then discovered the
event had been predicted " many years before
the king thought of it." [1] Bower was present
when a notable clerk revealed the prophecy.
The first abbot was Oswald of Germany, a man
of vast learning, and admirable sanctity ; the
second was Adam of Hangaldsid, a Scot who had
long lived in a monastery on the Continent, but
was allowed by the prior of the Grande Chartreuse
to go and rule the convent of Perth.

Sometimes more illustrious personages than
even Oswald and Adam arrived from the Continent to visit the King of Scotland. There
came one destined to leave his name in history,
and who was called Æneas Sylvius Piccolomini.
He had been sent by the Council of Basel, to
treat of certain religious matters. He was then
a very young man, among the most brilliant
Italy had produced. Learned, elegant, skilful,

[1] Appendix VIII.

filled with the spirit of the early Renaissance, a
lover of art, science, and history, a composer of
chronicles and romances, over-fond of those licen-
tious tales so much in favour in the lettered
courts of Italy, he was later to take holy orders
and to follow, not without fame, his new career;
he became Pope, under the name of Pius II.

The rudeness of the climate and manners
made a painful impression upon this elegant
nobleman, used to the refinements of marble
cities. He found in Scotland nothing but
material discomforts and physical annoyances.
He relates them at length; these unpleasant
recollections obliterate all others, so much so,
that after noting them all in detail, he fails to
tell us exactly what he came to accomplish in
the kingdom. Perhaps his mission was a secret
one; if so, the secret has been well kept. He
obtained, at all events, what he wanted : " Nihil
non impetravit ex his quæ petitum venerat."

Dreadful was his crossing, in the winter season, with two terrible tempests, " duabus maximis jactatus tempestatibus," one of them
lasting fourteen hours, and the other two nights
and a day. The ship was driven far away towards
the north, and the sailors, navigating under new
stars, ceased to know where they were : " Adeoque in oceanum et septentrionem navis excur-

THE PORCH OF WHITEKIRK.

rit, ut nulla jam cœli signa nautæ cognoscentes, spem omnem salutis amitterent." The passengers, believing themselves lost, made all manner of vows to the saints. Æneas promised to undertake a pilgrimage barefoot to the nearest shrine. The shrine happened to be that of Whitckirk, " Alba Eccelsia," as he calls it, near North Berwick.[1] The future Pope walked ten miles barefoot on the frozen ground, suffering such agony that on returning he had "to be borne rather than led by his servants."

After this beginning everything in the country seemed horrible to him. The days in Scotland, short enough in winter, appear to him shorter than they really are ; he only allows them three or four hours of light. He naturally mentions the poorness of the dwellings, greatly resembling those of to-day, built of stones, without mortar, and thatched with heather. The horses are hideous, he says ; they have shaggy coats, " never disentangled by iron brush or wooden comb." He wanted to see the famous trees which bore ducks for fruit, the said ducks, when ripe, falling from

---

[1] " The church of Hamer, which was dedicated to the Virgin Mary, was early called White-Kirk, from the whiteness of its appearance, and at length became in the popular tradition the name of the village and parish." N. Carlisle, " Topographical Dictionary of Scotland," 1813. The church still subsists.

the branches into the water and swimming away,
a sort of tree firmly believed in as late as the
seventeenth century ; but he was always informed wherever he went that they were to be
met *further off*, and he heard at last that they did
not grow in Scotland proper, but in the Orkneys.
One marvel, however, he saw and could testify
to. In this land " I saw at the church-doors
beggars, half-naked, go away happy after receiv-
ing pieces of stone for alms. This stone, owing
to the sulphureous or other fat substances contained in it, burns, and replaces wood, which is
lacking in this country." [1] A strange kind of
stone, truly, destined to work many wonders in
the world some day, being coal.

James did his best to cheer his guest, showing
himself courteous according to his wont ; he
presented the Italian with a couple of horses,
and there is no reason to suppose these had not
been carefully combed ; he also paid all his ex-
penses and gave him fifty nobles besides. But
all in vain ; the pilgrim of Whitekirk left with
a dreadful impression ; he described Scotland in
the darkest colours, and made matters worse by
praising England. Even James did not find
favour in his eyes ; he pronounced him heavy
and fat, very fat even, " multa pinguedine gravis,"

[1] Appendix IX.

an accusation which was keenly resented in Scotland when it was known there. " The Italians think us fat," the chronicler John Major indignantly answered, " because we are well fed ; people of the north have much flesh upon them, but there is no fat in it. . . . Those dry, bloodless Southerners rank as fat people those who have blood in them." "On the whole," continued Æneas, " Scotland and the border land in nowise resemble Italy ; it is a wilderness, which knows no sun at all in winter." [1]

[1] Appendix X.

VII.

SEVERAL other solemn embassies were sent
to James : by the Pope, whose encroach-
ments the Scotch king ever wanted to stop,
and with whom he had ever-recurring difficulties; by the King of England, who sent once
as an envoy Henry Beaufort, cardinal of St.
Eusebius, uncle of Queen Jane ; and by the
sovereigns of Europe, not without memorable
results. Charles VII. of France, hard pressed
by his foes, and as yet only " King of Chinon,"
felt urgent need of the help of his allies the
Scots ; a marriage might perhaps tighten the
bonds of this alliance, and a marriage was prac-
ticable, for he had a son Louis, dauphin of
Viennois, two years older than Margaret, eldest
daughter of James. He decided to despatch an
embassy to ask for the hand of the princess, and
he entrusted this mission to Regnault de Chartres,

Archbishop-duke of Reims, peer of France, and
to John Stuart of Darnley, "Constable of the
Scotch in France," belonging to the royal family
of Scotland, pensioned "as a reward for having
left wife and children," said the French King in
his charter, "to remain in the service of France."
This John Stuart, who, for the valour he displayed at Baugé and elsewhere, was made
Seigneur of Aubigny and Count of Evreux,
with the permission to quarter the arms of
France, was to die on his return from Scotland,
as well as his brother, at the battle of Herrings.
Both these ambassadors had orders to negotiate
the marriage, besides renewing " the ancient
alliances, leagues, and compacts existing between
the two nations as far back as the time of the
Emperor Charlemagne." They accordingly set
out towards the end of the year 1427, attended
by a large retinue, and travelling slowly, as
became personages of their rank.

A good diplomatist must know how to write
well and how to speak well. This was such a
recognised fact in the Middle Ages, that kings
often made their poets ambassadors owing to
the gift of eloquence bestowed on them by
heaven. Chaucer as envoy had represented
England ; Eustache des Champs, France ; Boc-
cacio, the Florentine Republic ; and Petrarch,

Padua. The unfortunate King of Chinon, shorn of all his territory, still possessed a poet and had recourse to him. While the archbishop and constable took their time, Charles despatched one more envoy, who was to precede them and prepare the way; and this envoy was none other than Maître Alain Chartier, " father of French eloquence," as he is called by Jean Bouchet, a peerless clerk and magnificent orator—" clerc excellent, orateur magnifique," says Octavien de Saint-Gelais in his " Séjour d'honneur."

Alain had lately returned from Germany on a mission to the Emperor Sigismund ; the mission had completely failed, without impairing Alain's renown in the slightest degree ; since a poet had not succeeded, it was plain no one could. Alain who, when abroad, translated his name into Latin, " Magister Allanus Aurigæ," [1] Master Alan of Carter, started accordingly, and went to seek James in his town of Perth.

---

[1] The names of the three ambassadors are given thus in James's letters patent concerning the betrothal of his daughter, and dated from Perth, July 19, 1428: " Reverendum in Christo Patrem Reginaldum permissione divina Archiepiscopum et Ducem Rhemensem, Parem Francie, Joannem Stewart, comitem Ebroicensem, dominum de Dernle, militem, consanguineum nostrum, et Magistrum Allanum Aurigæ, cancellarium Bajocens[em]." " Acts of the Parliament of Scotland," vol. ii. p. 27.

He was received in solemn audience. The
occasion was an important one, the eyes of two
nations were fixed on Alain. The man who has
expressed with happy simplicity many profound
truths, who has succeeded in giving a lasting
shape to many wise and ancient sayings, who
has been able to write sweet sentences, the glory
of our language, where not a word can be
touched, such as " La vieillesse vient tard aux
gens de modeste maison," Alain the poet kept
silence, and Magister Allanus Aurigæ, "ambaxi-
ator solemnis," spoke. The speech had been
composed beforehand, every word carefully
weighed ; a copy of it had been enrolled on
parchment, and thus we know to-day what the
ambassador said. As beseemed Magister Allanus,
his oration was a Latin one, and this is how the
"father of French eloquence " expressed himself
when he spoke Latin :

" Sire, when I behold myself, when I consider
the narrowness of my understanding, the paucity
of my eloquence, the exiguity of my person,
how dare I raise my eyes to such majesty, in
what terms begin my speech ; truly I know not.
Shall I rear to heaven my brow ; shall I venture
to set my taper near the effulgence of the sun,
and weary royal wisdom and learnèd ears with
my uncouth oration ? Distrusting my powers,

I would instantly forsake my task, did not the
thought of him who sent me, the object of my
mission, and your royal favour inspire me with
courage. . . . I have reflected how I might best
begin . . . and have found this mode of greeting
to be far above all others, and unsurpassable by
human ingenuity. . . . Thus, in the name of
the most Christian king of the French, your
brother, kinsman, and very dear ally, I address
your serene excellence in the words of greeting
used by the messenger Ahimaaz when he came
to King David and said : *Salve Rex !* " [1]

Many things are included in these two words.
What is a king, and what is a greeting ?
Allanus Aurigæ had not studied logic without
discovering that, in order to be understood, it is
necessary to be clear, and in order to be clear,
involved propositions should be reduced to their
essential parts. He therefore divides his propo-
sition in two parts, develops each of them in the
amplest fashion, every saying of his being
propped up by a quotation, so that by the time
the first half of his discourse is over, the king
and his court will have an exact notion of what
a king and a greeting really are.

Then by successive steps, with infinite pre-
cautions, he descends the long winding way that

----

[1] Text below, Appendix XI.

will bring him to his subject ; he dwells on the illustrious kingdom of Scotland and on the illustrious and unhappy kingdom of France. But in vain does he try when he arrives at that point to continue rhetorical, explaining to his royal hearer that " expectatio quasi enim ex spe statio derivata est," the eloquence of facts prevails, and there is something heartrending in this petition for his native land, still struggling against adversity, not quite overpowered, having lately gained some advantage over her foe—and who does not know that already, in the fields of Lorraine, the inspired shepherdess listens to heavenly voices.

Sentences follow each other, quotations begin again, the vision fades away. Whether owing to the eloquence of facts or of words is of little import ; certain it is that the speech made a great impression. When the archbishop-duke and the constable of the Scotch appeared on the scene they were received with due honour ; they were feasted, at a cost of £6 9s. 10d. [1] for one night, in the castle of Linlithgow (newly repaired by James), and they found no difficulty in coming to terms with the king concerning a

[1] " Et pro expensis domini archiepiscopi Remensis in Francia et domini de Derne factis una nocte apud Lithgw in eorum primo adventu, de mandato regis, testante camerario, vi £i. ix s. x d." " Exchequer Rolls of Scotland," vol. iv. p. 485.

definitive treaty. James set his seal to the deed at Perth on the 19th of July, 1428, and the original document brought over to Charles VII. by the ambassadors was ratified at Chinon on October 19th.

The object of this embassy, however, the Princess Margaret, was but three years old ; the Dauphin de Viennois but five. Years were suffered to glide by, and it was only in 1434 that the King of France sent another embassy to Scotland to fetch his son's betrothed. Alain Chartier had been dead some years ; so Charles decided to confide this important mission to his faithful councillor and master of the hostel, Regnault Girard, "knight, lord of Bazoges," a worthy and honest citizen, who, for all his knighthood, had small leanings towards adventures and navigations.[1] On hearing of the great honour thrust upon him, he almost fell ill. Troubled by the thought of the English fleet, and of tempests, he sought some way of

---

[1] His own account of the journey, with his instructions and a number of official documents, has been preserved, and is as yet unpublished. It is to be found in the MS. Fr. 17,330, No. 9, in the National Library, Paris. See "English Essays from a French Pen," 1896, pp. 24 ff. The mission of Girard, wrongly called Arnauld Girard and wrongly described as Governor of La Rochelle, "Gubernator Rupellæ," is mentioned in the "Liber Pluscardensis," 1877, vol. i. p. 374.

not stirring, and found no better one than to publicly offer four hundred crowns to any one who would go in his stead. Even in those days such a proceeding seemed unacceptable ; Charles informed his councillor that he must undertake the journey in person;[1] and to be sure he should not escape, sent the Comte de Vendosme to escort and see him safe on board. Regnault Girard, Seigneur de Bazoges, embarked thus on the 14th of November, 1434, "not," he says, in the relation he has left us of his journey, "without much sorrow and weeping."

Scarcely had the ambassador set sail, than his worst anticipations were fulfilled ; the sea proved as merciless to him as to Æneas Sylvius ; "a great and marvellous storm"[2] arose which lasted five days and five nights, causing him to miss the Scilly Islands, to miss Ireland, and be driven more than a hundred leagues off the coast, "according to the chart," into the "great ocean sea," on the way, though he knew it not, to the discovery of the New World. Regnault Girard,

---

[1] "Et estoit ladicte ambassade bien dangereuse et périlleuse. Et pour eschiver le danger de la mer, je voulusse donner quatre cens escuz à celluy qui entreprendroit l'ambassade et qu'il pleust au Roy me tenir pour excusé ; mais le Roy ne le volt consentir et me commanda très expressément d'aller en ladicte ambassade sur tout le service que jamais faire luy vouldroye." Fol. 120.

[2] See text, Appendix XII.

who had given himself up for lost before he even
started, was not, however, reserved for this
glory ; in his despair he had recourse, like Æneas
Sylvius, to a vow, and in his case too, the vow
was heard. More prudent than the future Pope
even in this dire necessity, the ambassador merely
promised a silver ship, with the arms of France
engraved upon it, to an Irish saint, and hastened
to offer his gift as soon as he landed.

After a journey of fifty-six days in the very
heart of winter and in stormy weather, " en fin
cueur d'hyver et en tourmente," Regnault Girard
could at last anchor before the rock and castle of
Dumbarton, or " Dompbertrain," as he calls it,
the chief port used for communication with
France in those days.   Once on shore, Charles's
councillor recovered his presence of mind,
negotiated skilfully, and overcame by his patience
and cleverness all obstacles.   These were many,
chiefly owing to the fact that the royal family of
Scotland was a most united one.   James and
Jane could not bear to part with their daughter.
They asked for guarantees and proposed con-
ditions.   A town of her own was to be assigned
in France to Margaret ; a Scotchman was to be
in command and the guard to be a Scottish one ;
the princess must have Scottish ladies with her
to keep her company : all this obliged Regnault

DUMBARTON.

Girard to write to his master and meant delays.
Then the king and queen would point out that
the time of the year was unfavourable ; " that
they could not send over my said lady the
Dauphiness at this season, for the Queen her
mother would never suffer it." And James
added, slily, " that we ourselves (the French
ambassadors) knew full well in what peril we
had been when coming to this said land of
Scotland." It was safer to wait till spring,
and then only would the youthful princess be
sent "à l'aventure de Dieu."

A delay of over a year was thus secured by
the king ; but February came at last, and the
treaty had to be fulfilled. A fleet sent from
France was waiting at Dumbarton to escort the
princess ; the hour of parting had struck.

The ambassadors and the royal family met
once more at a farewell banquet. Poor Jane,
in tears, was present, seated next the king " in
a chair." The following day " the King and
Queen of Scotland sent for the Dauphiness to
come before them, and addressed her in many
touching and memorable words, exhorting her
to behave rightly ; God knows what tears were
shed on both sides." No less affected than his
wife and desirous of endearing the whole family
to the ambassador who was to take charge of

Margaret, the king "ordered me, Regnault
Girard, to kiss the queen, and the queen kindly
and graciously saluted me ; which kiss I repute
the greatest honour ever bestowed on me. We
left thereupon."

Regnault departed to make all ready on board,
and remained at anchor fifteen days tossing on the
water, and enduring " great discomforts " ("où
j'enduray de grans malaises "), awaiting the king
and his daughter, who lingered, still anxious to
gain time. Presents were exchanged, those of
the ambassador being of primeval simplicity.
They consisted in "a gentle mule " (" ung mulet
bien gent "), offered by advice of the Comte de
Vendosme, and in six casks of wine, and three
of " chestnuts, pears and apples of divers sorts "
for the queen, "who was much pleased, there
being little fruit in Scotland." As for the mule,
it was considered " a very strange beast, because
there are no such animals over there." [1]

James arrived at last with the future Dauphiness ; wishing himself to select the ship which
was to carry his daughter, he caused the fleet to
put out to sea in his presence, " to ascertain
which was the swiftest and best appointed." It
happened to be a vessel of Spanish build, which
was at once chosen, to the great indignation of

[1] See text, below, Appendix XIII.

the Breton and French seamen, who rebelled and were with difficulty pacified.

The princess embarked, and the king, feeling there was nothing more in store save sorrow for all, shortened the final leave-takings, "did not stay long but went away weeping many tears" ("Le Roy n'y demeura pas longuement, mais s'en alla à grans pleurs, du regret de madicte dame la daulphine sa fille").

A century later the same harbour was to witness, under equally fateful circumstances, the departure of another princess of the house of Stuart : Queen Mary, then six years old, who left Dumbarton on a French galley to become, in her turn, Dauphiness of France, the first act in the tragedy of her life.

"On the fifth day of May, in the year fourteen hundred six and thirty, the town of La Rochelle was richly hung and decorated." Margaret of Scotland made a state entry therein. At Poictiers she was received by the mayor and notables, as well as by the doctors and students of the University ; while she was entering the town "a child, disguised as an angel, was let down from the portal of the city, and placed a chapel (crown) on her head, a thing which was most genteelly and craftily performed." Finally, Tours was reached, and there the gentle and

gracious Margaret, endowed, like many of the
Stuarts, with the gift of poetry, the heroine of the
legend of the kiss bestowed upon Alain Chartier
(who was dead, however, before she came to
France), married the Dauphin of Viennois, and
became acquainted with the husband Alain had
secured for her. He was the future King Louis
XI., who in truth, says Commines, "seemed
more fitted to rule a world than a kingdom,"
and who "loved no sport save hunting and
hawking in their season, but took not so much
pleasure in falcons as in hounds. As for ladies
he never cared for them."

Margaret did not find in her new home that
conjugal happiness she had been a witness of in
Scotland; the Dauphin never loved her. "When
he grew to man's estate," writes Commines of
his hero, " he was married against his will to
a daughter of Scotland, and as long as she lived
regretted it." The King and Queen of France,
on the contrary, worshipped her ; Charles made
her numerous presents ; we see him give to
" Madame la Dauphine on the first day of the
year, 1437, a gold mirror and stand set with
pearls." There exists a receipt delivered by
" us, Margaret, Dauphiness of Viennois," for
two thousand livres paid by Jacques Cœur, " we
being lately at Nancy in Lorraine, to purchase

cloths of silk and sables, to make robes for
our person." Margaret's nature was tender and
affectionate ; her husband's neglect, vile slanders,
caused her to fall into a decline ; and thus, on
the 16th of August in the year 1445, "at ten
o'clock of the night, she passed from life to death,
in the town of Chalons in Champagne," [1] the
childless wife of a heartless ruler of men. [2]

[1] "Lettres de Louis XI.," Société de l'histoire de France,
1883, vol. i. pp. 163, 201, 202.

[2] Appendix XIV.

VIII.

"WHOSO breaketh an hedge, a serpent shall bite him." James had reigned twelve years, and his iron hand had broken down many a hedge ; he strove to reconstruct and regulate, to reach the unattainable ideal for which his nation was as yet unfitted. After the bold enterprises of earlier years, always crowned with success, alarming symptoms began to show themselves. Dark prophecies flew from lip to lip, hinting that the love-tale, begun among the spring flowers long ago, would have a bloody ending ; omens multiplied in such a fashion that James himself, in spite of his optimism, could not help being struck by them ; a vague anxiety seemed to fill the kingdom.

Among the leaders formerly imprisoned, then set at liberty, figured Sir Robert Graham, crueller and fiercer than any of the others. Since his imprisonment vengeance had become his sole thought. He first endeavoured to foment a revolution, and to depose the king in the midst of Parliament. No less insinuating than audacious, he persuaded the nobles whose families had cause to complain of the king, that they ought to appeal to the monarch himself and oblige him to publicly recognise the wrongs of the Scottish aristocracy. He did more ; rising in the assembly where he believed his sentiments to be shared by most men, he walked to James "with a grete corage," and "sette handes upon the Kyng saying thes wordes, ' I arrest you yn the name of all the thre astates of your reume, here now assemblid yn this present parliament, for right as youre liege peple be bundun and sworne to obeye your Majeste noble riall, yn the same wise bene ye sworne and ensurid to kepe youre peple, to kepe and guverne youre lawe, so that ye do hem no wronge, bot yn all right mantene and defend hem.' "[1] It was a solemn moment, and all remembered the example of the Westminster Parliament deposing Richard II. But the two parliaments differed, as did also the two kings ; for when Robert Graham, turning to the Lords, added : "Is hit nat thus as I

[1] "The Dethe of the Kynge of Scotis," translated from the Latin by John Shirley ab. 1440 ; in Pinkerton's "History of Scotland," 1797, vol. i. p. 462.

say ?" instead of the unanimous assent of the
English Houses he received no reply, and his
words rang echoless through the assembly.

James had Graham arrested on the spot, in the
sight of the States, and led to a "sure and hard
prisone." So he thought at least; but treason
was in the very air. The great families he had
wished to crush made his government impossible ;
if he arrested a Campbell or a Macdonald it
sufficed that the lowest of the prison servants
should be a Campbell or a Macdonald for the
prisoner to be free. No bargain, no secret
understanding, no conspiracy was necessary, for
no oath was kept, no commands were obeyed,
which clashed with family claims. Following
his own impulse, without orders from any one,
the meanest of the *catervani* would risk death and
the awful tortures of the time to save the chief,
whatever his crime, without an instant's hesita-
tion : blood is thicker than water. The "sure
and hard prisone" did not long hold Graham,
who soon found himself free among the hills
" ynto the cuntreis of the Wild Scottis."

At first the king took little heed ; it was an
accident like unto many others, and he had too
many irons in the fire to be able to watch any of
them very closely. A Robert Graham was not
more to be feared than a Lord of the Isles, and

the Lord of the Isles had been recaptured, this time to be carefully guarded in the castle of Tantallon. But Graham was like no one else, and appeared hard even among men of iron. One day letters were brought to the king by a messenger from the remote Highlands. They contained a fresh challenge sent by Graham; he declared in solemn style, under his hand and seal, that having for his own part deposed the king, he considered him as a fallen monarch, shorn of the prerogatives of royalty ; and seeing in him only a man and a mortal foe, should kill him with his own hand as he would kill any of his foes. Let James Stuart look to himself! This was in 1435.

About the end of the following year, the king, having held his Parliament at Edinburgh, resolved to spend Christmas in his beloved town of Perth at the Blackfriars convent, where he often stayed. As he was about to cross the Scottish Sea, " the which is vulgarly clepid the water of Lethe," a wild looking woman, " that clepid herselfe a suthsayer," suddenly started up crying :

" My lord Kyng, and ye pase this water ye shall never turne ayane on lyve."

" Sheo nys bot a drunkine fule and wot not what sheo saith," observed one of the attendants of the king, who went on his way.

4

The Christmas festivities were very brilliant,
the king was surrounded by his family, the queen
being present, and all his court. Threatening
clouds gathered outside. A prophecy was cur-
rent which declared that in less than a year a
king should be slain in Scotland. James was
playing chess one evening with one of his
knights, surnamed for his pleasing manners
" The King of Love " ; and alluding, with his
unflagging gaiety, to the gloomy prediction, he
said :

" Sir Kyng of Love, hit is not long agone
sith I redd a prophecie . . . that this yere shuld
a kyng be slayne yn this land. And ye wote
well, Sir Alexander, there be no mo kynges yn
this reume bot ye and I ; and therfor I cownsell
you that ye be well ware, for I let you wit that
I shall ordeyne for my sure kepyng sufficiently,
I trust to God, so am I undir youre kynghood
and yn the service of Love." [1]

The company fell to talking of omens. One
had dreamed of the terrible Graham ; the king
confessed he too had had a dream—this time it
was not of the star-goddesses ;—he had been
attacked by a " cruell serpent and an horribill
tode " ; and being in his bedroom at night with-

[1] " The Dethe of the Kynge of Scotis," *ibid.* p. 466 ; see
below, Appendix XVI.

out any weapons, had fought against the reptiles
with the tongs.

Several weeks went by, and the Christmas
talk was forgotten. In spite of his boast the
king was no better protected than before. " He
never had guards near him," writes the chronicler, John Major, " by day or night, and it was
a great risk for a king who had put so many
nobles to death for their crimes." One evening,
the 20th of February in the year 1437, James
was once more seated at the chess-board, near
the fire ; the queen read a book of romance ;
others sang and harped. A knocking was heard
at the door, not the outer door of the convent,
but the door of the royal apartment. Who
could have gained admittance so late ? It was
the "suthsayer " woman, who had slipped by
unseen. " Let me yn Sire," said she, " for I haf
sumwhat to say and to tell unto the Kyng, for I
am that same woman that noght long agone
desirid to haf spokyn with hym at the Lith,
whan he shuld passe the Scottish sea." The
usher told the king of her coming ; but James,
who was playing, answered " Yea, let hir
cume to-morrow." The woman insisted, but in
vain. " 'Wele,' she said, ' hit shall repent yow
all, that ye wil nat let me speke nowe with the
Kyng.' Therat the usher lughe and held her

bot a fule, chargyng her to go her way. And
therwithal sheo went thens."

The night drew on ; the game being finished,
the king dismissed his friends, and, wearing
only a loose gown, stood before the fire, talking
with the queen. Without, all was dark and
still.

Suddenly torches flare at the windows, strange
noises are heard in the courtyard, hasty footsteps
on the stairs, the tramp of armed men, the mur-
mur of a throng. The hour is arrived, the
prophecies are come to pass, the sorceress had
spoken truth : the king was betrayed. Graham
was at the door with his rebel crew.

No means of defence, the king was unarmed ;
they rush to the windows, they had been
previously fastened, "strongli sowdid yn the
stonys with moltyne lede," the locks of the
doors were broken and the bolts removed. In
this emergency one of the queen's maids of
honour, Catherine Douglas, with a courage
worthy her name and race, thrust (it is said [1])
her arm through the staples of the door, and
while Graham was forcing his way in, crushing
her bones and flinging her bleeding on the
ground, James had seized the tongs, raised the
flooring, and slid into a dark hiding-place under

[1] Appendix XV.

the apartment. This vault gave access to the
moat, and through it the king might have
escaped. But Fate was on the alert ; three
days before, James, who often played tennis in
the moat, had caused the passage to be walled
up, because the balls were lost there : " Fortune
was to hym adverse." Endowed with great
muscular strength, he knocked down and half
strangled his first two assailants, but his hands
being cut by the daggers he attempted to
ward off, he remained defenceless, and soon
fell before Graham pierced by sixteen mortal
wounds.[1]

Thus ended the romance begun among the
spring flowers on a May morning. The queen
was wounded in trying to save the king, and
only escaped death by a miracle.

It has since been noticed that in the " Kingis
Quair," composed so many years before in
memory of happy days, James, as though moved
by a presentiment, had written these lines :

> And thus this floure, I can seye no more,
> So hertely has unto my help attendit
> That from the deth hir man sche has defendit.

Jane gave the king a last proof of her love, in

[1] Appendix XVI.

accordance with the customs of the period.
Having seized, after a hot pursuit, Graham and
all the assassins, she caused them to perish in
torments so atrocious that they were deemed
almost too cruel even in that age.

*   *   *   *   *

In the quiet retreat of the Library at Sienna,
adjoining the cathedral, can be admired the most
beautiful of Pinturicchio's paintings. Francis
Piccolomini, nephew of Æneas Sylvius, destined
in his turn to wear the tiara, ordered these
rescoes to be painted by the greatest artist of
his day. They represent the chief events of the
life of Æneas ; we behold him on his mission to
the King of Scotland ; James is there, portrayed
as an ideal monarch, wise and mild, with flowing
garments. A court of elegant noblemen sur-
rounds him ; kings of Love, who differ from the
one of Perth. And behind the throne, far as eye
can see, stretch the green hills and blue lochs of
an imaginary Scotland. The artist does not
show us the wild country where the pilgrim of
Whitekirk suffered so much ; unwittingly he
has painted the enchanted land where James

wandered in his dream, the river whose fish had ruby scales, the infinite blue of the Paradise where the King of Scotland had met Jane Beaufort.

APPENDIX.

I.

THE WILD SCOTS.

HERE is another testimony (of a later date) concerning the "Wild Scots." The southern inhabitants of Scotland are "assez civils" and they speak English; "mais ceux qui sont septentrionaux sont plus rudes, agrestes et fascheux, et pour cette raison sont appelez sauvages. Ils portent comme les Irlandois une grande et ample chemise saffranée, et par dessus un habit long jusques aux genoux, de grosse laine, à mode d'une soutane. Ils vont teste nue et laissent croistre leurs cheveux fort longs et ne portent chausses ne souliers sinon quelques uns qui ont des botines faictes à l'antique qui leurs montent jusques aux genoux.

"Leurs armes sont l'arc et la flesche et quelques javellotz qu'ils tirent fort dextrement, et une large espée avec le poignard pointu, qui

ne taille que d'un costé. Ils sont fort légers a
la course . . . Tous ces sauvages parlent
Irlandois." " Navigation du roy d'Escosse
Jaques cinquiesme du nom autour de son
royaume . . . soubz la conduicte d'Alexandre
Lyndsay excellent pilote Escossois, recueillie
. . . par Nicolay d'Arfeville . . . premier cos-
mographe du Roy," Paris, 1583. Nicolay,
whose work is partly translated from "un petit
livret escrit à la main en langage Escossois,"
received by him from " milord Dudley" in
1546, describes himself as having spent part of
his life " abandonné à mille manières de dangers
ès contrées estranges par mer et par terre."

II.

THE TRUCE BETWEEN ENGLAND AND SCOTLAND,
1404–5.

A TRUCE had been concluded in 1404 "atte
castel of Pountfreyt, the sixte day of Juyl,
the yeer of our lord Jesu Crist a Thousand
foure hundred and four," between English and
Scottish commissioners who decided " that fro the
twentyth day of this presente moneth of Juyl,

the sunne rysyng, until the day of Pasque next
folowand, the sonne goinge doun, shall be kept
trewly and effectuali Trieues generales by land
and by see, between our foresaid Liege lord the
kyng of Scotland, for hym and his Roiaume of
Scotland, his landes, lordshippes, lieges and soubgitz on that on part, and his adversaire of
Engeland, his Roiaume of Engeland, lands,
lordshippes, lieges and soubgitz on that otheir
part." Ratifications were granted by the King
of Scotland on the 20th of August and by the
King of England on the 18th of September,
1404. "Fœdera," 3rd. ed., vol. iv. pp. 68 ff.
Same statement in Andrew of Wyntoun, who
affirms, as well as Bower, that the capture took
place during the truce :

> Trewis bath on sé and land
> Wes takyn for to be lestand
> Tyll evyn on the next Pasch day
> Fermly festnyt on all gud fay.

"Orygynale Cronykil of Scotland," ed. Laing,
Edinburgh, 1879, vol. iii. p. 96. Bower says :
" Et quamuis paulo ante trevæ erant tunc inter
regna tam per mare quam per terram captæ, in
Anglia nihilominus per octodecim annos prin-
ceps detentus erat et captivatus apud eos."
Continuation of Fordun's "Scotichronicon,"

1759, vol. ii. p. 439. Walsingham refers the
event to the year 1406 ; he says that there was
a truce then ; but only a truce on land, not by
sea. He wants obviously to exculpate Henry
IV. as much as possible : if the date of the
capture was really 1406 he had a better excuse
to offer in favour of the English king, for there
was no truce at all then. This seems to point to
1405 being the real date. Though some excellent authorities such as Sir W. Hardy accept the
statement of Walsingham, the question remains,
to say the least, an open one ; we have no
charter or positive evidence to settle it, and
Walsingham does not seem to have been par-
ticularly well informed in this special case.
Some of the circumstances he relates, and the
order of his facts (death of Fleming) are
undoubtedly erroneous. It is not unlikely that
Wyntoun will in the end prove right.

III.

KING JAMES'S POEMS.

A VARIETY of poems have been attributed to
King James ; the authenticity of them all
has been disputed. The principal minor works

with which he has been credited are "Christis
Kirk on the Green," "Peebles to the Play,"
"Song on Absence," and a "Ballad of Good
Counsel" : this last, a short poem of 21 lines,
is considered as authentic by Mr. Skeat (see his
"Kingis Quair," Scottish Text Society, 1883–4,
the best edition of that work). All the others
are certainly not by King James. The "Kingis
Quair" had, up to a very recent date, escaped
the fate of the other poems attributed to him ;
but that time is over, and Mr. J. T. T. Brown
has just tried to establish in his "Authorship of
the Kingis Quair," 1896, that this poem is also
an apocryphal work. His thesis, though very
cleverly defended, is, I believe, untenable ; I
have given my reasons for this belief in a letter
to the *Athenæum*, Aug. 15, 1896. See the corre-
spondence between Mr. Brown, Mr. Skeat, Mr.
A. H. Millar and myself in the *Athenæum*, July
11 to Aug. 29, 1896.

The "Kingis Quair" exists in only one MS.
(Arch. Selden, B. 24 in the Bodleian Library,
second half of the XVth century, written by a
Scotch scribe). It is there attributed, both at
the beginning and end of the poem, to "King
James of Scotland ye first" ; to " Jacobus primus
Scotorum rex illustrissimus." The testimony of
the MS. is fully borne out by John Major, the

historian and professor of logic, the most critical
and best informed of the old historians of Scotland,
who says in his "Historia Majoris Britanniæ,"
printed in Paris, 1521 : "Artificiosum libellum
de Regina, dum captivus erat composuit, ante-
quam eam in conjugem duceret" (fol. cxxxv.).

Bower does not mention the poem, which
seems not to have been publicly known in the
lifetime of the king ; but he speaks of the
intellectual attainments of James, and says the
king followed all sorts of literary pursuits :
"operi artis literatoriæ . . . complacenti instabat curæ" (below App. VII.). The words
used by Bower had in the Middle Ages a very
comprehensive meaning and included all that we
consider now as belonging to literature, be it
poetry or prose. John of Salisbury, wanting to
extol the manifold virtues of Grammar, and
show that it is the source and nurse of all
philosophy and all literature uses the same
expressions : "Eadem [Grammatica] quoque est
totius philosophiæ cunabulum et (ut ita dixerim)
totius literatorii studii altrix prima."—"Opera
Omnia," ed. Giles, v. p. 34.

IV.

JAMES'S TREATIES WITH NORWAY AND HOLLAND.

"Fecit enim multa bona in vita sua, regno perpetue profutura. Unde cum sibi constiterat regnum Noricis obligari pro insulis in inæstimabilem summam, a multis retroactis temporibus insolutam, misit rex suum militem intimum dominum Willelmum de Creichton et magistrum Willelmum Fowles, custodem sui sigilli privati, cum honorabili familia, regi Norwegiæ in ambassata; ubi sic per instructionem et industriam regis actum est quod de præteritis quitantiam reportarunt, et ab hinc solveretur tantum annuatim nisi summa centum librarum sterlingorum.

"Fecit etiam pacem inter regnum nostrum et Hollandos, qui, ante reditum ejus de Anglia, mercatoribus Scotiæ intulerunt innumerabilia damna." Bower, in his continuation of Fordun's "Scotichronicon," ed. Goodall, Edinburgh, 1759, vol. ii. p. 509.

V.

SOME OF KING JAMES'S LAWS.

On Private Wars.—"Tha na man tak on hande in tyme to cum to amuff (excite) or mak weire aganst other under payne that may folowe be course of common lawe."—Parliament of Perth, 1424-5.

On the Help to be provided for the King.—"Gif ony disobeyis till inforse the kyng aganst notoure rebellouris aganis his persone quhen thai be requiryt be the kyng and commandit thai shalbe chalangit be the kyng as fautouris of sic rebellyng bot gif thai haif for thame resonable excusacion."—Same Parliament.

Against numerous Retinues.—"Item it is statut that na man of quhat estate, degre or condicioun he be of rydande or gangande in the cuntre leide nor haif ma personis with him na mai suffice him or till his estate and for the quhilkis he will mak full and redy payment."—*Ibid.*

On Salmon.—"Item quha sa ever be convickit of slauchter of Salmonde in tyme forbodyne be the lawe he sall pay xls. for the unlaw and at the thride tyme gif he be convickit of sic trespasse he sall tyne (lose) his lif or than by it."—*Ibid.*

Against Football.—"Item it is statut, and the kyng forbiddes that na man play at the fut ball under the payne of iiij*d.* to be raysit to the lorde of the lande also as oft as he be tayntyt (convicted) or to the sheref of the land or his ministris gif the lordis will not punishe sic trespassouris."—*Ibid.*

On the Practice of Archery.—"Item it is ordanyt that all men busk thame to be archaris fra thai be xij yeris of eilde. And that in ilk x £i worth of lande thar be maid bowmerkis and specialy nere paroche kirkis quhare upon haly dais men may cum and at the lest schute thrise about and haif usage of archary."—*Ibid.*

Against Rooks.—"Item forthy that men consideris that rukis bigande (building) in kirkisyardis orchardis or treis doith great skaith apone cornis it is ordaynt at thai that sik treis pertenys to lat thame to byge and suffer on na wyse that thar birdis fle away, and quhar it be tayntyt that thai bige and the birdis be flowin and the nestis be fundyn in the treis at beltane the treis salbe forfaltit to the king. . . ."—*Ibid.*

On the Royal Law.—"It is ordanit be the king with the consent and deliverence of the thre estatis that all and sindry the kingis liegis

of the realme leif and be governyt undir the
kingis lawis and statutis of this realme alanerly
(*i.e.,* all anerly, only) and undir na particulare
lawis na speciale prevalegis na be na lawis of
uther cuntreis nor realmis."—Parliament of
Perth, 1425-6.

On the Repairing of Castles.—" It is ordanit be
the king and the parliament that ever ilk lorde
hafande landis be yonde the mownthe (*i.e.,* the
Grampian mountains) in quhilk landis in aulde
tymes thare was castellis, fortalycis and manis
placis, big, reparel and reforme thar castellis and
maneris and duele in thaim be thaim self or be
ane of thare frendis for the graciouse governall
of the landis be gude polising and to expende
the froyte of thai landis in the cuntre quhare the
landis lyis."—Perth, 1426. " Acts of the Parliament of Scotland," 1814, fol. vol. ii.

VI.

A FIGHT BETWEEN HIGHLANDERS.

" CONFLICTUM est acriter apud Stranavern
inter Angusium Duffi et Angusium de Mur-
rave, qui paulo ante carceres regis evase-

runt, libertati donati. Cum utrolibet summa-
batur de catervanis mille et bis ducenti, et hi
omnes una die mutuo se mactabant. De tanto
numero vix vivi novem personæ evaserant. De
quo non modicum multis est mirandum, quod
ita animose sese impeterent, quod nullus ad
salvandam vitam suam fugæ beneficio se muniret.
Quod fit ideo, quia nostri Scoti transmontani in
confino sive marchia mundi constituti, parum
sentiunt de torrida æstate sive solis æstu quo
sanguis amicus naturæ siccaretur : et ideo inter
cæteras nationes mundi audaciores naturaliter sunt
reperti."—Bower, *ibid.*, p. 491.

VII.

THE PASTIMES OF JAMES I.

" Hic etenim in musica, non solum in sono
vocis, sed et in artis perfectione, quemad-
modum in tympano et choro, in psalterio et
organo . . . natura ipsum decoravit, præsertim
in tactu citharæ tanquam alterum Orpheum. . . .
In hoc patuit ipsum naturalem fore Scotum, ipsos
etiam Hibernienses in modulationibus lyricis
mirabiliter præcellentem. . . . Nunc operi artis

literatoriæ et scripturæ, nunc protractioni et
picturæ, nunc in jardinis herbarum et arborum
plantationi et inserturæ, nunc honestis ludis
et solatiis, ad refocillandum suorum sequacium
animos, sine offendiculo, complacenti instabat
curæ. . . . Incredibili æstu amabat scientiam
scripturarum. Amabat et exercitium diver-
sarum et laboriosarum practicarum. Unde
translatus in Angliam, tanquam alter Josephus
ductus in Ægyptum, etsi linguam quam non
noverat audivit, artes tamen mechanicas et
scientias morales quas non noverat, didicit et
intellexit."—Bower, *ibid.*, pp. 504, 505, 506.

VIII.

CONCERNING CARTHUSIANS.

"Sunt, sicut audivi, nonnulli, qui derogant
isti sanctissimo ordini ; quia, ut allegant, non
audiverunt de miraculis eorum de ordine,
sicut et de aliis sanctis aliorum ordinum. Nec
mirum : quia, in quantum possunt, hujusmodi
celant, soli Deo placere desiderantes ; et ideo
dubitare de sanctitate vel puritate ordinis, non
solum est sacrilegium, sed blasphemum. Quia

si istud est dubitare, est etiam dubitandum an
beatus Johannes Baptista qui hanc vitam eligit
et duxit, sit sanctus. . . . Unde sciendum est,
quod miracula communiter fiunt ad probandum
sanctitatem illius qui ea fecit, quando aliquod
dubium potest insurgere circa sanctitatem ejus.
. . . Non legimus Johannem Baptistam in vita
sua aliquod fecisse miraculum ; cum tamen inter
natos mulierum major eo non surrexit."—" De
fundatione Cartusientium apud Perth in Valle
virtuosa." Bower, in his continuation of Fordun's "Scotichronicon," Edinburgh, 1759, 2
vols. fol., vol. ii. p. 492.

IX.

ÆNEAS SYLVIUS'S IMPRESSIONS OF SCOTLAND.

" Scotia ejus insulæ in qua est Anglia suprema
portio est, in Aquilonem versa, fluminibus
haud magnis et monte quodam ab Anglia dis-
creta : hic nos brumali tempore fuimus, cum
sol paulo amplius quam tres horas terram
illuminaret. Jacobus eo tempore regnabat quad-
ratus et multa pinguedine gravis. . . ."

James, after his return from England, " com-
plures regulos gladio percussit. . . ."

" Audieramus nos olim arborem esse in Scotia,
quæ supra ripam fluminis enata, fructus produ-
ceret [anserum] formam habentes, et eos quidem
cum maturitati proximi essent, sponte sua decidere,
alios in terram alios in aquam, et in terram
dejectos putrescere, in aquam vero demersos mox
animatos errare sub aquis, et in aere plumis
pennisque evolare. De qua re cum audivimus
investigaremus, didicimus miracula semper re-
motius fugere, famosamque arborem non in
Scotia, sed apud Orcades insulas inveniri. Illud
tamen nobis in Scotia miraculum repræsentatum
est. Nam pauperes pene nudos ad templa
mendicantes, acceptis lapidibus eleemosynæ
gratia datis, lætos abiisse conspeximus : id genus
lapidis sive sulphurea sive alia pingui materia
præditum, pro ligno, quo regio nuda est com-
buritur." " Æneæ Sylvii Piccolominei. . . .
Opera quæ extant omnia."—Basileæ, fol. " De
Scotia," p. 443.

X.

JOURNEY OF ÆNEAS SYLVIUS TO SCOTLAND.

(Æneas speaks here in the third person.)

"Navem ingressus, dum Scotiam petit, in
Norvegiam propellitur, duabus maximis jactatus
tempestatibus, quarum altera quatuordecim
horas mortis metum incussit, altera duabus
noctibus et una die navim concussit, atque in
fundo perfregit, adeoque in Oceanum et Septentrionem navis excurrit ut nulla jam cœli signa
nautæ cognoscentes spem omnem salutis
amitterent : sed affuit divina pietas, quæ sus-
citatis aquilonibus navim ad continentem repulit,
ac duodecimo tandem die terram Scotiam
patefecit : ubi apprehenso portu, Æneas ex voto
decem millia passuum ad beatam Virginem
quam de Alba Ecclesia vocitant, nudis pedibus
profectus, cum illic horis duabus quievisset,
assurgens moveri loco non poterat debilitatis
atque obstupefactis hiemali frigore pedibus.
Saluti fuit nihil edendum illic invenisse, atque
in aliud rus migrandum fuisse : quo dum famu-
lorum ope magis portatur quam ducitur, pede-
tentim terram quatiens calefactis pedibus ex

insperato sanitate recepta ambulare occepit. Ad regis denique praesentiam intromissus, nihil non impetravit ex his quæ petitum venerat ; sumptus ei viarum restituti sunt, et in reditum quinquagenta nobilia, ac duo equi quos gradarios appellant, dono dati.

"De Scotia hæc relatu digna invenit. . . . Subterraneum ibi esse lapidem sulphureum, quem ignis causa defodiunt ; civitates nullos habere muros, domos magna ex parte sine calce constructas, villarum tecta de cespitibus facta . . . equos natura gradarios omnes . . . neque fricari equos ferro aut ligno pecti, neque frænis regi . . . nihil Scotos audire libentius quam vituperationes Anglorum . . . silvestres Scotos lingua uti diversa . . . hiemali solstitio (tunc enim illic fuit) diem non ultra quatuor horas in Scotia protendi."

He returns home by way of England:—

". . . Ad Novum Castellum pervenit, quod Cæsaris opus dicunt : ibi primum figuram orbis et habitabilem terræ faciem visus est revisere : nam terra Scotia et Angliæ pars vicina Scotis, nihil simile nostræ habitationis habet, horrida, inculta atque hiemali sole inaccessa."—"Pii Secundi . . . Commentarii rerum memorabilium."—Frankfort, 1614, fol., p. 4.

XI.

ALAIN CHARTIER'S SPEECH TO JAMES I.

"Dum ad me ipsum reversus, sensus penuriam, inopiam sermonis et mee tenuitatis indignitatem meditatus sum, qua audatia in tantam majestatem oculos convertam, quibusve vocibus loqui aggrediar nescio. Os in celum ponam et candelulam inter solis splendores efferam, dum regiam sapienciam et doctissimorum audienciam rudi et indocto sermone fatigabo ? Jam ego diffusus viribus, operis resilirem si non mittentis digna gratitudo ac rei de qua agitur honestas, daret fiduciam, vestra regalis clementia, serenissime princeps et rex illustrissime, audaciam confortaret . . . Cogitavi idcirco ex verbis ordiri que non loquentis studio, sed sua propria suavitate grata sint, indignumque os loquentis dignificent. Ejusmodi sunt verba salutis, quibus nichil excellentius proferri, nichil alcius potest hominum intelligencia meditari. . . . Nomine igitur christianissimi Francorum regis, fratris, consanguinei et confederati carissimi, serenitatem vestram excellentissimam alloquor verbo salutis quo Achimias nuntius allocutus est David, dicens : Salve Rex. (R. xviii.) Hec brevis oratio duo com-

plectitur : verbum quod inter spirituales actus
sanctus resonat cum dicitur Salve, et nomen
virtutis in terris celsitudinem enuncians tem-
poralem, dum subjungitur Rex," etc.—(MS. Lat.
8757, fol. 47, in the National Library, Paris ;
the MS. contains various dialogues, letters, and
discourses, "venerabilis viri magistri Alani
Quadrigarij," and other works, *e.g.*, a "De
Curia Fortunæ " by Æneas Sylvius.

XII.

REGNAULT GIRARD AT SEA.

"ITEM et ledict jour quant feusmes prestz et
appareillez, mondict seigneur de Vendosme et
ledict Jehan Chasteigner nous feirent l'honneur
de nous venir conduire par terre jusques au
droict de Chef de Boys estant de ladicte ville
une lieue ou environ et tous les gens d'estat de
ladicte ville de la Rochelle jusques au nombre
de cent ou six vingtz chevaulx, et à tant
priasmes à mondict seigneur de Vandosme qu'il
luy pleust nous recommander à la bonne grâce
du Roy, et illec prismes nostre congé pour aller
à nostre navire et ne fut pas sans deul ne sans

grans pleurs de part et d'autre. Puis entrasmes
en ung bateau pour aller en ung baleiner nommé
Marie qui estoit à moy Regnault Girart, dont
estoit maistre, emprès Dieu, Tassin Petel, et
estions en nombre tant de gens de terre que de
mer soixante et trois personnes ; et aussi vint
avecques nous Puver et sa nef chargée de mar-
chandise, lequel Puver estoit du navire pour
amener madicte dame.

"Item, le jour suivant avecques la benysson
de Dieu prismes nostre temps et feismes voyle
de la marée du soir, et le xviij^{me} jour dudict
moys nous trouvasmes à l'isle de Sorlingues à
heure de deux heures après minuyt ; et illec
soubdainement nous prist si grande et mervil-
leuse tormente que ne peusmes recouvrer l'avre
de ladicte isle ne aussi recouvrer la terre d'Illande. Si nous convint, par le conseil des marcans prendre la grand mer oscéan. Et nous
dura ladicte tormente cinq jours et cinq nuyctz,
et nous jecta par delà les Ilandes selon la carte
plus de cent lieues. Et par force de ladicte
tormente escartasmes la nef dudict Puver. Et
ladicte tormente cessée retournasmes vers Illande
et le xxiiij^e jour dudict mois de novembre, par
la grâce de Dieu arrivasmes au bout d'Illande à
ung très hault et merveilleux rocher nommé
Ribon qui est le bout de toutes terres devers ouest

et est terre inhabitable, et illec getasmes l'ancre
à l'abri dudict rocher.   La tormente nous reprist
et demeurasmes cinq jours à nous défendre contre
la tormente, mais nos ancres et nostre cordage
furent trop grandement endommagez.   Et le
xxixme jour d'icelluy moys de novembre, par le
conseil des marcans, prismes l'adventure de nous
couler et maroyer selon la couste d'Illande."—
MS. fr. 17330, No. 9, in the National Library,
Paris, fol. 216.

A hundred years later another Frenchman,
famous since, Pierre de Ronsard, came as a
young man to Scotland and experienced the
same dangers from the adverse elements.   He
mentioned in several of his poems his journeys
to Scotland and the breaking of his ship.   He
was sent, he says, in one of his elegies by the
Duke of Orléans to Flanders,

> Et encore en Escosse, où la tempeste grande
> Avecques Lassigni cuida faire toucher,
> Poussée aux bords anglois, ma nef contre un rocher,
> Plus de trois jours entiers dura ceste tempeste,
> D'eau, de gresle et d'esclairs nous menaçant la teste.
> A la fin arrivez sans nul danger au port
> La nef en cent morceaux se rompt contre le bord,
> Nous laissant sur la rade, et point n'y eut de perte,
> Sinon elle qui fut des flots salez couverte,
> Et le bagage espars que le vent secouoit,
> Et qui servoit flottant aux ondes de jouet.
> D'Escosse retourné, je fus mis hors de page.

(Elegy XX., to Remy Belleau).

XIII.

REGNAULT GIRARD LEAVES SCOTLAND—A FAREWELL BANQUET AND AN EXCHANGE OF GIFTS.

"Et pendant ledict temps ledict Roy d'Escoce feit ung banquet et nous y manda et, pour honneur du Roy, nous feit seoir à sa table et la Royne près de luy sit en une cheyre. Et fut ordonné que nous Regnault Girard, Aymery Martineau et Joachim (son of Regnault Girard) yrions à Dombertrain pour ordonner sur le faict du navire et ledict Hue ·Crennedy demourroit pour adviser et advancer le faict de l'armée.

"Le jour suyvant emprès ladicte ordonnance ainsi faicte audict lieu de Sainct Jehan Stoun (*i.e.*, Perth), lesdicts Roy et Royne d'Escosse feirent venir en nos présences madicte dame la daulphine et luy dirent plusieurs beaux motz et notables eu luy remonstrant l'honneur du prince avec lequel elle devoit estre esposée et en la inhortant de bien faire ; et Dieu sait les grans pleurs que d'une part et d'autre estoient faictz en cette matière. Et ce faict, prismes nostre congé, et ledict Roy, pour honneur du Roy de France sondict frère, commanda à moy Regnault Girart bayser la Royne, laquelle de sa grâce et

humilité me baysa, que je répute le plus grand
honneur qui oncques m'advint. Et à tant nous
despartismes.

"Item, le jour suyvant, en nostre logis dudict
lieu de St. Jehan Stoun, ledict Roy nous envoya
de grans dons, et si ne faict pas à oblier que
depuis que nous arivasmes audict Royaulme
d'Escosse devers luy en sa ville de Edembourg,
qui fut le xxvᵉ jour de janvier, l'an mil
iiijᶜ xxxiiij jusques à ce que prismes nostre congé
de luy audict lieu de St. Jehan Stoun, qui fut ou
mois de fevrier mil iiijᶜ xxxv, nous feit deffrayer
et paier nostre despense ordinaire quelque part
que feussions en sondict Royaulme.

*   *   *   *   *

"Item, pendant le temps que je estoye sur la
mer, sur l'ancre, vint une nef de France laquelle
me apporta des vitailles et par dedans y avoit ung
mullet bien gent lequel j'avoye faict venir par
le conseil de mondict seigneur de Vandosme qui
le me conseilla quant il me mist à la mer, car
il avoit veu le mulet à la Rochelle, et pour le
donner audict Roy d'Escosse, lequel mulet je
luy feys présenter et en fut molt joyeulx et fut
chose bien estrange de par delà, pour ce qu'il
n'en y a nulz. Et aussi feys présenter à ladicte
Royne d'Escosse trois pipes plaines de fruict,

tant grosses chastaignes, poyres et pommes de diverses manières, et aussi six pipes de vin, de quoy la Royne fut bien contente, car de par delà il y a bien peu de fruict."—*Ibid.*, fol. 141 and 142.

XIV.

DEATH OF MARGARET, DAUGHTER OF JAMES I., DAUPHINESS OF FRANCE.

"Heu proh dolor! quod me operteat scribere quod dolenter refero de ejus morte, cum mors . . . eandem dominam . . . brevi dolore eripuit . . . Nam ego qui scribo hæc vidi eam omni die vivam, cum rege Franciæ et regina ludentem, et per novem annos sic continuantem. Postea . . . vidi eam . . . in casula plumbea in ecelesia cathedrali dictæ civitatis Calonensis, ad cornu magni altaris ex parte boriali, in quadam tumba posita[m] ; rege dicente quod post pauca tempora levare faceret eam, et apud Sanctum Dionisium inter reges et reginas universas ibidem collocari. Cujus epitaphium sequitur, consequenter hic, quod super ejus tumbam positum fuit post mortem, in lingua Gallicana ; modo hic in lingua Scoticana translat[um], ad præceptum inclitæ memoriæ regis Jacobi secundi fratris ejusdem dominæ. Incipit . . ." (Here follows a poem of several pages). F. J. H. Skene, "Liber Pluscardensis," Edinburgh, 1877, vol. i. p. 381.

XV.

THE "BAR-LASS."

CONTEMPORARY writers are silent concerning the famous deed of the "bar-lass," the best known, but least certain, of all the incidents in the king's eventful life. Bower never mentions her ; the account translated by John Shirley (see following note) credits a lady of the name of Douglas with great intrepidity ; but she is called Elizabeth, and the part she plays in the drama is different. Hector Boece, who wrote in the following century (and who allowed room for many fables in his book) gives the often repeated story : "Itaque is extemplo interfectus, eam tamen moram præbuit ut ostium accurrente Catharina Douglas nobili adolescentula, quæ postea Alexandro Louel à Bolumme nupsit, clauderetur. Verum pessulo magno, opera Johannis illius aulici cujus modo meminimus, ablato, quum ad manum nihil esset, manum in foramen præstantissimo animo inscruit. Sed confracto brachio tenello videlicet ac fragili, atque virgine repulsa in cubiculum invasere." "Scotorum Historiæ . . . Libri," Paris, 1574, fol. 353 (1st ed., Paris, 1527). Drummond of Hawthornden commemorated in the same way the deed of "a maid of honour of the name of Dowglass" ("History of Scotland," London, 1655, fol. p. 31). Most historians since have done the same. Catherine was the subject not only of Rossetti's well-known poem, but also of a drama : "Catharine Douglas, a tragedy" (verse and prose), by Sir A. Helps, 1843.

XVI.

THE DEATH OF JAMES I.

THE most detailed account we have of King James's murder is to be found in the little tract entitled, "The dethe of the Kynge of Scotis." It was translated from the Latin in or about 1440, by John Shirley, the famous book collector and admirer of Chaucer. It has been printed by Pinkerton in his "History of Scotland, from the Accession of the House of Stuart," London, 1797, 2 vols. 4to, vol. i. p. 462, and by J. Stevenson, " Life and Death of King James I.," Glasgow, Maitland Club, 1837, 4to. It ends thus: "And thus nowe here endethe this most pitevous cronicle of th' orribill dethe of the kyng of Scottes, translated oute of Latyne into oure moders Englishe tong bi youre symple subget John Shirley, in his laste age, after his symple understondyng." Shirley was then over seventy. Pinkerton says the " Latin relation " translated by Shirley was "probably published in Scotland by authority." This does not seem very likely. The writer, of course, pities the king very much, and calls Graham a traitor ; but he seems to find in his heart a good deal of admiration for the pluck of the traitor, and to discover many things to blame in the king. Graham is "a man of grete wit and eloquence" ; he accuses James "with a grete corage" ; he defends himself "with manly hart" ; while James is described as "noght stanchid of his unsacionable and gredi avarice," and as levying undue taxes. The conclusion and moral of the story is thus recorded: " Therfore prynces shuld take hede, and drewe it to thare memorie of maistre Johanes de Moigne (*i.e.*, Meung, the author of the " Roman de la Rose ") counsele, thus

said yn the Frenche langage : ‘Il n'est pas
sires de son pays, quy de son peple n'est amez.’”
The writer, in fact, concludes against James ;
so that if the pamphlet was “published by
authority,” that authority was certainly not a
very friendly one.

Long before becoming the subject of Rossetti's
“King's Tragedy,” the death of James was
poetically told in the “Myrroure for Magis-
trates,” 1559. There the feeling runs very
high against him and against Scotland ; the
object of the poem is to show “how King
James the first, for breaking his othes and bondes
was by Gods sufferauns miserably murdred of
his owne subjectes.” He is represented as taking
a very optimistic view of his capture by “good
King Henry,” and of his captivity :

> For ere I had been a prisoner eyghtene yere,
> In which short space two noble princes dyed . . .

he was released. He swore fidelity to England,
but allowed himself to be persuaded—

> To helpe the Frenchmen then nye overtrode
> By Englishmen.

He was, therefore, forsaken by God and
killed by “Robert Gram.”

Unwin Brothers,

THE GRESHAM PRESS,

WOKING AND LONDON.

By J. J. JUSSERAND.

ENGLISH ESSAYS FROM A FRENCH PEN. Illustrated. Cloth, 7s. 6d.

Times :—" M. Jusserand's book is full of varied interest, and we need not say that such intrinsic interest as it possesses is greatly enhanced by the literary skill with which the writer presents his matter, and the scholarship with which he elucidates it."

A LITERARY HISTORY OF THE ENGLISH PEOPLE, from the Origins to the Renaissance. Cloth, 12s. 6d. net.

Daily News :—" Probably M. Jusserand has written the best extant book on the early literature of our country."

Times :—" The work is full of rare attraction. . . . English readers will study it with profit and delight."

Daily Chronicle :—" The marvellous story of our literature in its vital connection with the origin and growth of the English people has never been treated with a greater union of conscientious research, minute scholarship, pleasantness of humour, picturesqueness of style, and sympathetic intimacy."

LONDON : T. FISHER UNWIN.